Scavengers
of the
Southwest

J. Oliver Johnson

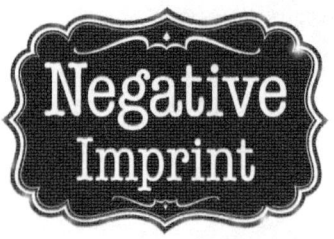

Once, if my memory serves me well, my life was a banquet where every heart revealed itself, where every wine flowed.

One evening I took Beauty in my arms — and I thought her bitter — and I insulted her.

Arthur Rimbaud, from *A Season in Hell*

PROLOGUE

There's a story the old-timers tell out there in the desert about a mysterious vagabond with a silver sock who met his fate someplace along a stretch of US-95, probably somewhere just a click or two up past Searchlight.

The story never tells how the stranger arrived, or from where he first stepped out. But the tale's generally always the same, regardless of who the storyteller might be, how mush gusto they put into spinning in, or whether or not they really believe in the tired old legend.

There's a stranger — a traveler, just some wayward no-account drifter with no stated home or destination — and he's got an accent and a very particular style of dress and mannerisms that none of the local townspeople can place anywhere specific. Even the worldliest and most well traveled find the vagrant odd and misplaced in normal society.

He appears suddenly in front of the Chittenpük, an old general store of sorts — what folks nowadays might refer to as a convenience shop. The building is small, set up along the narrow blacktop ribbon just far enough away from the previous stop to act as a last chance supplier of the bare essentials, like gasoline or Dr Pepper, or maybe some of those chocolate-covered insects displayed on the store's counter as a novelty impulse buy to long-distance motorists. One can never tell, after all, when they may come across another roadside Native American buffalo jerky stand before they get to where they're going.

It's not unusual that nobody would have noticed the stranger's arrival. Patrons are few and far between, though the merchandise price markup, which is grumbled at by customers but still expected, keeps the little store in business with no nearby competition.

The shop's counter is tended to most nights by an elderly clerk who passes the time by flipping through the pages of a dirty magazine or trying in vain the manipulate the rabbit ear antennas atop an old television set, just trying to find a channel that won't simply tell him how hot and dry it is beyond the shatter-resistant panes of glass at his back.

That old shopkeeper's face is worn and grimy,

crusted a bit around his eyes and forehead with the sweat and tears he perspires while silently berating himself for having not skipped town decades ago to take a chance on the lights and dreams of that pop-up city the mob built just a bit up north.

On other days, the shop is manned by a younger generation. This one occasionally goes into the city for a taste of excitement, but he always returns to the Chittenpük, vowing to one day stay up there for good, to break the cycle of boredom so that his future kids might know a life with luxuries like swimming pools and central air-conditioning. He dreams away the workday — planning, scheming, studying to earn a liberal arts degree online from the University of Phoenix.

Maybe he'll put his education to good use one day, expand the family business, become CEO, open up a Chittenpük-themed casino on the strip. Or maybe he'll just remodel the flagship location to include a sandwich counter featuring fresh-baked gluten-free bread.

The stranger has brought with him a gunnysack, which he's tossed down at his feet just outside the entrance to the Chittenpük. On his feet are holey hiking boots, his blackened toenails visible in some places through the worn boot leather. Completing the ensemble are filthy jean shorts that used to be pants; a faded yellow t-shirt, cut off just above the bellybutton, that advertises a previous year's pancake festival in some unheard-of Oregon town; and a blue bandana tied Axl Rose-style over a matted mop of dirty blond. In his left hand is the sock, the longer tube variety, formerly white with blue and yellow stripes at the top but now permanently encrusted with a sticky silver colorant.

The hobo stands near the door of the general store, mostly mumbling incoherently to himself, but louder when he finds an audience in a family of passersby who want nothing more than to use the restroom facilities, fill up the gas tank, and maybe peruse the selection of Ben & Jerry's. He holds his hand out, expecting something to be given to him, and he makes a noise that sounds almost like a string of words that trail off to an emphasized end that might suggest a question is attempted.

Quarter for the men's room?

Some customers politely ignore the stranger, while others scramble back into their station wagon and chance the distance to the next filling station. Eventually, someone phones the authorities.

As a pair of police officers arrives in their patrol car, the filthy tramp scoops up his dusty gunnysack and attempts to make a quick break of the area. *But where to?* In a dazed panic, he sprints in short circles around his original loitering spot until finally tripping on the curb and slamming his unshaven face down against the cement. He whimpers, motionless, eyeing the half of a tooth that has broken off and is now lying four inches from the tip of his nose. Snot bubbles form and then pop, speckling the concrete

4

directly in front of his pungent breath with tears and blood and little silver flakes.

The cops look to each other for explanation, but all they can offer one another is an identical shrug of the shoulders. They look toward the shopkeeper through the dusty store window, but he's oblivious, uncaring, lost in the pages. They grasp the vagrant by the arms and bring him to his feet.

"Pain," the dirty alien mumbles. "Pain."

"Well, yeah," one officer sympathizes. "You took quite a tumble there. How 'bout we take you in and have you looked at?"

"Pain," the bum repeats.

"What's that you got there in your hand?" the other cop asks. "Is that a sock?"

"Fo da pain," the weirdo slurs.

"It's for the pain?" the first cop searches for clarification.

"Nuh-uh," the dirty man explains. "Da *pain*."

He clumsily unslings his gunnysack and begins to rifle through its contents. The officers each take a couple of steps back and place their right hands at their holsters, unsure of the hobo's intentions. After a few seconds, the stranger slowly produces from his bag an aerosol can, which he promptly sprays into the fabric of the crusty tube sock. Then he places the opening of the sock over his mouth and nose before inhaling the resulting fumes.

"See?" the vagabond smiles. "Fo da pain."

"For the *paint*," the second cop nods. "This guy's

a fuckin' huffer."

"Goddamn junkie," his partner agrees.

The officers snatch away his sock and spray can, stuff them into the old gunnysack, and then cuff the stranger's wrists behind his back without much physical protest from their perp.

On their drive along the asphalt back toward the stationhouse, the high sun is characteristically baking the sheet metal of the patrol car. In the distance, the officers don't even notice the dancing waves of bent air along the surface of the roadway.

The blacktop is known to sometimes melt in these parts, or just crumble at the soft shoulder and tumble in chunks into the desert sand. Locals often just drive along the center stripe to avoid the torn edges, moving easily back into their own right-hand lane when opposing traffic nears.

The day of the stranger's appearance is especially hot. A scorcher. It's the kind of day when folks think to carry in their car an extra gallon or two of water. But the officers never expected to be called away from the office. When they received the call, they figured they'd give a hitchhiker a ride to the bus terminal, maybe slip him some charity in the form of fare to Phoenix, and then they'd head back indoors to crank up the AC and put their boots up on the desk.

The angry sun is vicious that afternoon, and it easily overtakes the weakened comfort of an expected leisurely drive back into town, even with the vehicle's windows rolled up and the air-conditioning unit straining to push coolness out through the dashboard vents. The cloudless sky encroaches upon the car's interior, highlighting the gunnysack that sits atop the back seat behind the driver.

As the hobo presses his sunburnt face against the window of the right-rear door, his belongings bake, and the fumes rise out through the bag's fabric. The stranger doesn't notice — or maybe he welcomes the vapors. His caretakers don't notice the fumes by their smell, but they begin to sense the effects.

"I'm feeling a bit light-headed," the driver admits with a sigh.

"Turn the AC up," his partner suggests.

But that just makes matters worse. The fumes invisibly circulate throughout the vehicle's cabin, and the car's three occupants continue to breathe the vapors in, and then back out. Huffing in, and then back out. From the spray can and the paint-soaked sock, up into the vents, blown around again into the trio's lungs.

The cops have each driven these roadways a couple million times. They grew up here. They know the back roads and the shortcuts through the desert. They know where to speed up and slow down to properly execute the tight corners and avoid the ravines and gulches.

On any other day, there'd be no reason for the cruiser to crash. There'd be no reason for the patrol car to slip down off the long unpaved shortcut path that runs perpendicular between two other marked blacktop streets and come to a sudden halt, smashed nose-down in a massive ditch against a boulder of brown granite.

The officers hold on for a while, maybe an hour or so, bleeding out from their wounds and succumbing to massive head trauma inflicted by the steering wheel and dashboard. They never even feel the impact, nor do they ever awaken from it. Their passenger, however, has been somewhat cushioned during the collision against the backs of the front seats.

The stranger slips his cuffed wrists down his back and maneuvers his legs through so that his hands are back in front of him. Genuinely concerned for their wellbeing, he nudges each cop, trying to wake them up.

"We can't park here," he mumbles to no response. "You're gonna get a ticket."

He slings his gunnysack over his head and climbs up through the broken rear window, then sits a while atop the trunk lid, which rests upright several feet below the edge of the gulch. The stranger removes his bag, then searches through it for his tiny tube of Testors brand airplane cement. He looks over the mangled wreck from his perch, contemplating his options.

"Not enough glue to fix it," he slurs. Then he removes the cap, inserts the tip into one nostril and inhales deeply.

It's the kind of situation that nobody can survive

for very long. No water, no food, no escape from that damned sun. For the lucky victim, someone eventually finds their petrified corpse. But for most people, the critters pick apart the meat and drag the bones away. The sand blows through and covers up the remaining evidence, and whatever's left of the physical being is consumed by the desert forever. In a hundred years' time, someone might stumble across the car while excavating for the basement vault of a brand new hotel and casino.

It's not a pleasant story, but it's still told on occasion nonetheless, usually by some old-timer who swears he knew someone who actually encountered the stranger that day long ago. It's become folklore, an urban legend, a myth — just like the story about the five-foot-tall armadillo that mutated from the nuclear bomb testing, or the one about all those raspy-voiced ghosts walking the halls of the old MGM Grand.

They'll tell you that, even to this day, if you drive out there in the desert on certain nights when there's a gentle breeze, just past that old gas station that sells edible insect-based snack foods, you can still smell the faint ghostly fumes of a tube sock soaked in silver spray paint, and you can hear the voice of that wayward drifter whispering something incoherently to anyone who believes enough to listen.

Quarter for the men's room?

1

I was tooling along the main drag on the north side of the city when the hunger became too strong to ignore any further. As I randomly poked at the radio station preset buttons, searching for something other than bubblegum pop, across the street from me appeared a Del Taco, whose sign broke through the skyline of pawn shops and budget hotels on the less glamorous side of town.

I'd just flown in on a flight originated at the Philadelphia airport, with an extended layover in Dallas, but I was finally at my destination. I hadn't eaten since the night before and I feared my stomach was turning on itself. I knew that it was only a matter of time before my abused and neglected liver and kidneys also took up hostile action.

I stomped my right foot down hard onto the accelerator, and with all four cylinders working to their full potential, I ripped the steering wheel to a hard left and shot the hatchback rocket ship across the busy lane going my direction along my port side. The little car jumped the center divider and narrowly avoided collision with coupes and limousines alike. I miraculously passed through the southbound traffic without so much as a scuff on the fire engine-red exterior of my rented ride, then hopped the curb of the shopping center parking lot and skidded to a halt beneath the towering sign of the Mexico-inspired fast food eatery.

I had an acquaintance waiting on me just up the road, but he'd been waiting on me since the day before and a few more minutes wouldn't kill him. I once ate five Del Taco quesadillas in just under two minutes, and all I wanted this time was three.

"Time me," I commanded a young Asian girl as she retrieved empty plastic trays from atop a nearby trashcan. She might not have understood English well because she returned a look of confusion before hurrying back behind a door marked *Employees Only*. "Never mind," I grinned to the empty dining area as melted cheddar and greasy tortilla slid down the inside of my neck. Less than five minutes after arriving at the restaurant, I was back on the road.

"Where the hell have you been all day?" my companion asked impatiently after I screeched the car to a halt in front of the cheap hotel he'd stayed at his first night there. He looked tired, ragged, as if he'd slept in his white linen shorts and sky-blue polo shirt before hopping straight out of bed and scurrying off to the strip for excitement and breakfast. "I've been calling your cell phone for hours!"

"I had trouble at the car rental agency," I explained.

And that was no lie. I specifically asked the man behind the counter there for a big red convertible, the older the better. *How else could I cover something like this righteously?* But the only convertibles they had were Mustangs, and they were all blue or silver, and they were rather expensive. I had to settle for a brand new Nissan Versa with just enough cargo space for two moderately sized suitcases. I went in looking for a Great Shark, but I drove away in a Minnow.

"Well, I'm hungry," my friend snapped at me. "All I've had to eat today was a six-pack of Coors. I got it from a little store down the road, and I had to walk all the way there in flip-flops. I also bought a bottle of water to counter the dehydration, but I gave it to some bum I met in front of the store. His name was Scruff. He was a friendly man, not like those asshole bums I saw during my layover in San Francisco. I never even got anything to eat while I was in California."

"Let's check in to the hotel first, and then we can go find somewhere to eat," I assured him. "I know of a Del Taco just down the road from here."

"That's not a good idea," Hank warned. "As your

doctor, I advise you to limit yourself on your quesadilla intake while we're here. You know you're lactose intolerant, and I don't wanna be responsible for having to call your mother."

Hank wasn't really my doctor, or *any* doctor for that matter. He was just a biology student with dreams of attending medical school at some point in the future, which is the closest thing to a doctor I could find on such short notice. And in my line of work, having a personal physician on hand could be a life-saving decision. Plus, I knew he was good people.

I had met Hank Matthews more than ten years earlier in a crowded shower in San Diego. There were probably thirty men stuffed into that shower at the time, and a short Mexican named Chavez had just asked if he'd really just seen me piss on the shower floor.

"Well, that depends," I answered. "Were you staring at my penis?"

"Touché," Chavez admitted. He made a quick exit and I could sense somebody else creeping up on me from behind.

"Hey, I like your tattoos," Hank's deep voice casually informed me. Somehow, that conversation starter seemed stranger than the one I'd just endured from the guy who admitted to checking out my privates.

Hank was a Louisiana boy, I was from central California, and we were both fresh out of high school.

We were recruits attending boot camp for the United States Marine Corps. After breezing through three months of basic training, we were both sent to Florida for air traffic control school.

Once there, we made separate friends and our paths rarely crossed until I found myself confined to the barracks due to a disciplinary issue. I had been informally questioned by the local civilian law enforcement as part of their investigation into the death of a bartender from an establishment some friends and I were known to frequent often. Though someone else later admitted to strangling the poor girl and tossing her body from a Pensacola bridge, underage drinking was still considered a serious enough offense in the military and I found myself temporarily restricted to my room. I was allowed to leave only for school, meals, or cigarette breaks in the smoke deck outside the ground floor of the barracks.

"I heard you killed a hooker," Hank inquired one evening as we each lit up a Marlboro.

"Nah, she was a bartender," I corrected him. "I've got orders to Yuma after graduation. Where are you going?"

"Same."

Marine Corps Air Station Yuma, Arizona was where they sent those Marines who either pissed off the higher-ups or were simply terrible at their designated occupation. Receiving orders to Yuma was a form of punishment, a *go to hell* from those who assigned the orders, or a *fuck you* from angry folks with the shiny emblems on their collars.

In a matter of weeks, Hank and I were both in that southwest corner of Arizona, within walking distance of both California and the border to Mexico. We spent our on-duty hours talking to airplanes from inside the air traffic control tower overlooking the Marine Corps base and what technically passed for an international airport.

With the lives of so many military and civilian pilots and passengers in our hands, it was a job that required the utmost skill and focus, which was hard for us since we spent most of our off-duty hours once again boozing it up in the sleaziest of dive bars, since those were the establishments that catered to underage heavy drinkers.

Lance Corporal Matthews was washed out from the career field first, considered by his supervisors to be unable to properly handle the duties of an air traffic controller. I, while probably equally inept at the job, lasted a bit longer than he did. It wasn't until I was deemed responsible for causing a near miss between an AV-8B Harrier jet and a Ford Explorer that my superiors decided to "shit can" me before I actually killed someone.

That was about a month after those hijackers steered a pair of passenger jets into a couple of skyscrapers in New York, and both the military and the FAA had to take a more scrutinizing approach in ensuring the competency of everyone involved in air travel. Hank was reclassified as an aviation supply clerk and I was on my way to an unwanted job as a military policeman.

By chance, I found myself at a Lynyrd Skynyrd concert in the parking lot of the local Indian casino a few months later, sitting next to the master sergeant in charge of the base public affairs office, which was responsible for putting out the military installation's weekly newspaper. After pretending to know something about journalism and impressing him with my extensive knowledge of the Lynyrd Skynyrd band, the master sergeant agreed to let me write a space-filler newspaper story about a barbecue one of the squadrons was having. Since I spelled most of the words correctly, and since the public affairs office was desperately short-manned at the time, the master sergeant pulled some strings and got me permanently assigned to his office as a military journalist. It was a career move that I welcomed whole-heartedly, and one that would ultimately change the course of my life.

Writing isn't for everyone. But for those who truly enjoy such work, who put their very soul into what they create, there is nothing else for them to do but write. There's a certain brand of freedom inherent in the task, even when assigned a topic so bland you know it will find no readers.

A painter could maneuver his brush in such a way, and choose his colors based on his mood at that very moment in time, to make a masterpiece of what could very well have been garage sale fodder by someone operating with less heart. Likewise, a musician can pluck the strings with a certain precision and accentuate his vocals with such vibrato as to create an anthem that might have otherwise been relegated to campfire fare if his mood during creation had been less passionate. Writing is no different an art form. The chosen words and the manner in which they're strung together is like paint on canvas, like a song in the air. That drive to write, to create this art, can be enough to sustain a person, or at least define his character.

"I'm gonna drink until I shit myself," my physician growled as we barged through the entrance of the Circus Circus and weaved our way up the ramp to the second level of the casino. "We really should've brought some ether, or maybe some mescaline."

"You watch too many movies, you poor fool," I snapped as we came upon the upstairs bar area. "This is it."

"I thought it was called the Carrousel Bar," Hank whined. "The sign says it's the Horsearound Bar. Are you sure this is the right place?"

"Yep, I check it out online," I reassured him. "I have the Internet on my cell phone. Same bar, different name."

The bar was closed, but we sat down anyway, hoping the bartender was simply on a break. We sat there smoking our cigarettes while ponies stuck to metal poles spun slowly around us. I took Hank's cell phone from atop the bar and convinced some thin middle-aged woman with dirty-blond hair and four young kids in tow — one of which was leashed to her belt with a bungee cord — to take our picture using the built-in camera. After obliging our request, she quickly handed back the phone and chased her untethered children into the midway.

"What the hell were you thinking?" my doctor scolded me after the woman was out of hearing range. "She could've stolen my phone. Then what would we have done?"

"Well, the kid on the leash would've slowed her down, so we could've caught up with her. No problem."

"Then what? We couldn't just let her go. What kind of example would we be setting for her kids?"

"Shit, you're right," I agreed. "You might've had to slit her throat. Did you bring your pocket knife?"

"No, they wouldn't let me bring it in my carry-on. Said I'd have to check it, but that would've cost me fifteen dollars. So I just gave the knife to the girl behind the counter."

"Well, no worries," I assured him. "You could've just used your belt. Asphyxiation is painless, or so I've heard."

"No way, man. I couldn't do that to those kids!"

"Who said anything about killing her kids, you sick fuck?" For a student of biology, he surprised me sometimes with his thoughtlessness.

"Gentlemen, please," a woman beckoned us

from outside the slow-whirling carrousel. "The bar is only open on Fridays and Saturdays, so I'm gonna have to ask you to leave. And please lower your voices; this is a family establishment."

"Holy fuckin' Christ!" I sputtered as I finally noticed the grossly unfair ratio of children to drunkards present. "Where'd all these goddamn kids come from?"

"Please, sir," she continued. "One woman has already complained."

Uninterrupted, I turned back to my companion. "Well, we'd just have to take that woman's kids down to the Encore, pretend we work there and hand the children out as door prizes. We'd pass the whole operation off as some new marketing technique. Nobody will question us. People trust the management there."

"Steve Wynn's a fuckin' genius," my doctor declared. "He invented Las Vegas as far as these people are concerned."

"Jay Sarno can rot in hell for turning the Strip into a goddamn daycare center. Fuckin' Grandissimo. Let's get the hell outta here."

We took the car to some cheap hotel just off of the main drag. We were working-class people, after all, and were on a very tight budget. As we checked in, we asked the elderly woman behind the counter if the pool was functional.

"Yeah, I guess so, but you really don't wanna swim in it," she warned. "There was a bit of a mishap in there recently — a fecal mishap — and I'm not entirely convinced the sanitation process was conducted properly."

"What a bummer," my doctor lamented.

"And there's no smoking allowed in the rooms," she continued, more sternly now. "And don't you guys even think about disabling the smoke detectors or pissing in the sink."

"Not us," Hank grinned. "We're responsible people."

"And cigarette smoke dries out my eyes," I added. "It's even worse out here in the desert. The sides of my eyes get red and cracked, full of gunk. It's fuckin' disgusting."

"This man suffers from a bad heart," Hank explained for me. "Angina pectoris. But we've got plenty of medicine, yes we do."

"I really have that, you know," I informed my phony physician, in all seriousness. "Angina pectoris is a real thing."

"Really? Did they give you plenty of medicine for it?"

"Nah," I shrugged. "I took some water pills for a little while to help reduce the sodium, but that's about it. I just have to eat better, exercise more, shit like that."

"How cute," the desk clerk interrupted, obviously wanting to get back to her soap operas on the miniature black and white television behind her. "And will you be needing one bed or two?"

"Which one costs less?" Hank inquired, that cheap bastard.

"Are you guys on drugs?" the lady asked, peering at us carefully over her thin-framed glasses. "Because we won't tolerate any of that either."

"No, of course not," I reassured her. "He's simple; it's not his fault. And despite what my friend's choice of apparel might suggest, we'll be sleeping in separate beds. Also, do you know if Debbie Reynolds is in town? We used to romp with her."

"I believe she's dead, sir," the woman said, still with no emotion attached. "Or she might just be in Reno."

"What about Danny Gans?"

"I take it you guys don't follow the news."

"Never mind," I conceded. "Which way to our room?"

We were situated on the second floor, the view of the Vegas skyline obscured almost completely by dilapidated structures. But at least we could see the car. As we unpacked our bags, I remarked about how this trip would be a whole lot better with acid and asked Hank what he had brought with him.

"I have some uppers in the brown bottle in my shaving kit," he said, trying to get into character.

"Brown bottle?" I began rummaging through the small bag he had placed on the bathroom counter. "This is vitamin B!"

"You won't need much," he warned, "just a tiny taste. Your body won't be able to properly metabolize any more than one tablet, so taking any more than that wouldn't really help you anyway. You'd just piss it all out."

"B vitamin? You fuckin' rat bastard! How the hell can we handle something like this with a clear head? You're supposed to be my doctor, goddamn it. You, of all people, should have known better."

Back in the car, Hank demanded to hear some

music while we started our adventure. I pushed the button on the CD player and the most horrendous sounds ripped from the speakers. It sounded like some sort of foreign-language dance rap, as if Tiny Tim had covered an obscure early Enrique Iglesias number, but then Kanye West remixed it. I punched the button and ejected the CD, which must have been forgotten by the previous driver. Hank immediately launched the compact disc out the passenger-side window of the speeding car as if trying to score a long Frisbee golf hole-in-one.

"Incubus," he said, sliding the band's recently released album into the dash-mounted stereo. "Just what the doctor ordered."

Before the player had time to read the digitized music, I again smacked the eject button and launched that disc past Hank and out his window.

"What the hell!" he screamed at me. "I just bought that. You owe me twelve dollars!"

"Fuck that. I just did you a favor. We need to hear the Stones. *Beggars Banquet.* Let's crank this shit up to maximum volume." I slid in another CD, and just as "Sympathy For The Devil" began to pick up momentum, that psychotic doctor of mine snatched it out from the player and flung it too out the window.

"Now we're even, you fanatic asshole," he screamed, still burning me with his resentful eyes. "Serves you right. What else did you bring?"

"I brought the Wallflowers, but it's still in my suitcase. All I have in the car is a Skynyrd compilation

I made. That's all I brought with me."

"Pre-crash?"

"No, *1991* and forward."

"So no 'Curtis Loew.' Fuck that."

I backhanded Hank hard across the lips. "You shut your goddamn mouth, you fuckin' pig!"

"Fuck!" Hank began pressing his fingertips to his face, then checking them for signs of blood. "What the fuck is wrong with you? You hit me!"

As he checked his face for bruising in the mirror on his door, a brown leather hiking boot stomped the side of Hank's head, and then kicked the mirror from the side of the car, leaving it dangling from a wire.

"Pull over, you punk bitches!" yelled the angry driver of a white Jeep with no roof or doors. He was racing alongside of the Minnow, yelling all sorts of obscenities at my doctor. "Pull the fuck over! You like throwing shit? I'm gonna throw you, motherfuckers!"

"What the hell is that?" I screamed at Hank. "What the fuck have you done this time?"

"You hit my Jeep with those fuckin' CDs," the shirtless sixty-year-old man was yelling, his wild hair blowing behind him like the cape of some comic book super villain. "I'm gonna skull-fuck you faggots!"

The sweet sounds of Journey blared loudly from the Jeep speakers, but the vocal power of Steve Perry was no match for this psychotic throwback from the Woodstock era. On second thought, this man would have been too violent for Woodstock. He'd have been more likely responsible for inciting the terror at Altamont.

"Turn here, left," Hank commanded at the next intersection, but the white Jeep followed closely. His engine was twice as big as ours, and jumping through traffic was our only defense.

I felt like Steve McQueen in *Bullitt*, except all McQueen had to deal with was guns and the hilly streets of San Francisco; I had bumper-to-bumper traffic and intoxicated jaywalkers to worry about.

I zipped quickly behind a stretch limo, and then a party bus, and then ahead of a motorcycle. I could see the Jeep get lost in the traffic behind me, eager to break through and narrowly avoiding several fender-benders. In a matter of time, we were far ahead of him, the motor of the little Nissan wound up and sounding like a weed whacker on nitrous oxide. We were lost, somewhere behind the Wynn, twisting through parking lots and small side streets, grinding the wheels on curbs until we finally emerged back on the Strip.

"As your doctor, I advise you to drive as fast as you possibly can toward Fremont Street." Hank was nervously looking over both shoulders, hanging onto the side-view mirror to prevent it from clanging against the door. "That fucker will never think to look for us there."

We found an empty spot in the corner of the fifth level of the El Cortez parking structure, then we walked briskly through the casino toward the exit onto Fremont Street.

"Now *this* is Vegas," Hank said, putting his nose into the air and inhaling deeply as we shuffled past the geriatrics shoving coins into the slots. "We can stay in here all day and avoid all the tourists."

"You asshole," I reminded him, "you're a fuckin' tourist."

I needed fresh air. That place highly reeked of stale piss and formaldehyde, but my doctor was convinced it was simply rotting flesh.

"Look over there," he said, pointing to a corner. "It's the mummified corpse of Bugsy Segal. They use

26

it at as a tourist attraction. Come on; I'm hungry."

I wanted a burger and a Coke, but my physician was already homesick and pointed out a restaurant that served Louisiana food. He clasped onto to my elbow and pulled me toward it.

"Well, alright then," I mumbled.

I let my coonass doctor order for me, essentially ensuring I'd get an authentic New Orleans dish all the way out there in the Las Vegas desert.

"And can I get you guys something to drink with that?" smiled our attractive young waitress.

"Yeah," Hank answered, getting back into character. "Two Singapore Slings with mescal on the side, and beer chasers.

But after noticing the confused look on the server's face, he changed the order to two Budweisers in tall glasses.

"So, what's this assignment you're working on?" the doctor inquired while studying the derrière of the young waitress as she sauntered back toward the kitchen. "Who hired you?"

"Nobody yet," I explained.

I had come out here to this desert oasis not for play but for a chance at proper employment. I had caught wind, from all the way out on the east coast, of some new start-up online Vegas magazine that needed to staff their entire office as quickly as possible. Everything's going digital, their website explained, and physical newspapers and hardcopy magazines are becoming a thing of the past. So some rich young assholes from somewhere nearby in California sank their parents' money into this journalistic venture in hopes of running the entire thing over the Internet.

"They'll have news, features, current events, advertisements, horoscope, comics, classifieds, letters-to-the-editor — the whole nine yards," I explained to Hank. "But it's all online, so there's very little overhead."

"So where do you come in?"

"Well, they're gonna need some writers, editors, photographers — a whole staff, basically. So I padded my resume, forged some documents and got an email back from one of the guys in charge. They want me to do a write-up on a weekend in Vegas, from the perspective of both the tourist and the resident. You know, something everybody can relate to. They want to show people that Las Vegas isn't just what they show in the movies."

"What the fuck are they talking about?" Hank slammed his fist on the table. "The movies only show the *best* parts of Vegas!"

"I know, but you have to give the editors and publishers what they want. And if they like my work, they'll hire me on the spot. Then I can move the family out here, finally escape from the stagnant American Dream, just live it up out here inside this bubble, unaffected by anyone else's expectations or reality television. Las Vegas is exempt. It's for people who want an alternative to everything else. This is, after all, where the American Dream came to die. At least that's what the book said."

"But are you sure they'll hire you?"

"Goddamn you, man!" I scolded, pounding my own fist on the table. "Do you realize who the fuck you're talking to?"

I stopped yelling because the waitress was back with our beer and food.

"What the fuck is this?" I asked her after she put a bowl of something down in front of me.

"It's what you ordered, sir," she calmly said. "Or what he ordered for you."

"It's Cajun food," my doctor interrupted. "You'll like it, trust me. And you'll never find it up there in New Jersey. I'm actually surprised we found it out here in the middle of the desert. Try it, man. When in Rome."

"But we're not in Rome, you fucktard," I countered. "We're in Las fuckin' Vegas, and I want a one-dollar hotdog and a thirty-ounce margarita."

But the food was already there, so I ate it. It wasn't bad — not good enough to entice me to pack my stuff and move down the road from ole Amos Moses, but it was certainly edible. We ate our meals, finished off a couple of beers each, then we took a stroll down Glitter Gulch.

"Pull over," I slurred, grabbing onto my doctor's shoulder for stability. "I need to puke."

"You're walking," he said, flinging me off his arm toward a freestanding trashcan. "Jesus Christ, that stuff got right up on top of you, yes it did. How much did you have to drink?"

"Two beers? I can't remember," I said, still needing my doctor's assistance as my legs were now unable to work properly.

Terrible things were beginning to happen inside of me — my stomach was twisting around and my intestines were burning, my skin began to glow a deep red and my temperature spiked to where I could actually feel my hair burning. I latched onto the side of the trashcan, as both my equilibrium and my vision were becoming questionable. It reminded me of the time I accidentally overdosed on niacin dietary supplements, except this was far worse, possibly fatal. I pried the lid from the garbage bin and fell frontward into it, my head hovering inches above a half-eaten hotdog from an A&W joint. I came up only when I was void of my thirty-seven-dollar lunch.

"What the hell happened to you?" My doctor pulled me out from the can and steadied me against the side of it. "New Jersey's really messed you up."

"I guess I'm just not used to the desert anymore. I've been away for too long. Maybe it's too hot for me now. I just had to get that beer outta my belly."

But I was still far from alright. My eyes were glowing red — even I could see that — and my entire body was pouring sweat, even more so than the average tourist there under the shade canopy erected high up above Fremont Street. A few steps from the trashcan and less than twenty yards from where I had eaten the meal, the bad feelings came back again, and so my head went back into the bucket.

"Geez, your friend is really fucked up," said a voluptuous woman, aged forty-something, in a pink tank top and black mini skirt. "Bad acid?"

"No, bad beer, I guess," my doctor explained to her as she laid her palm against my brow.

"Goddamn, he's on fire! You can fry an egg on his forehead."

"Back off, harlot," I slurred at her. "You keep your rotten eggs away from me."

I was foaming at the mouth and falling over more as Hank tried desperately to hold me up without making it appear as a homoerotic embrace. The woman's friends, who were waiting unhappily several feet away, called for her to leave us alone.

"Just a minute," she told them before turning her attention back to us. "Those are my girlfriends. My divorce was just finalized, so we all flew out here from Chicago to celebrate."

"Hey, you're divorced, too?" Hank had just taken a new interest in the lady. "Maybe you and I should go off and get married while we're here. I haven't done *that* in Vegas yet."

"Leslie!" Her heifer friends were hungry and tired of waiting on her.

"Alright," she said, "I gotta go, but we'll be back here later tonight. If you get bored, come on out and maybe we'll run off and get married. And put your friend there in bed; it looks like he might be allergic to something."

"It's quite alright, ma'am," he told her. "I *am* a doctor, you know."

"Slut!" I tried to yell at her, but I think I may have been the only one to hear me. "I need to sit down." But there were no benches anywhere, so I found another trashcan and leaned myself against it. My doctor's attention was still on the woman.

"What do you think? Should I just get drunk tonight and marry her? She was into me, I could tell. And she looks pretty good for her age, right?"

"Yeah, she was pretty hot. And maybe she has a daughter your own age. Let's get back to the room. I might be dying. You can help me write up my will, but you're still not getting a goddamn thing."

Not wanting to chance me puking inside the El Cortez and enticing Jackie Gaughan to have us taken out the old-fashioned way, we walked past the entrance and on down to the eastern end of the block to the parking garage.

"I think there's something wrong with me," I mumbled as I threw the car key at Hank. "Why don't you drive." I slouched down in the passenger seat and closed my eyes. I was out before he put the car into reverse.

I woke up to Hank opening up my car door and letting me fall out onto the scorching blacktop of our hotel parking lot.

"Motherfucker," I growled.

"I stopped at a gas station to fill up the Minnow and I picked up some supplies while we were there."

"Supplies?"

"Yeah," he said, showing me a thermometer he picked up from the medicine aisle. "And as your doctor, I'll need to take your temperature, so open up your mouth." Still motionless and on my back, I opened up and he slid the thermometer under my tongue. "Jesus Christ, it's a hundred and four!"

"I'm lying in the sun, you asshole. Get me inside."

After pulling me to my feet, he helped me to the stairs, but I could walk better now than before.

"You need to puke some more?

"No, I don't have anything left in my stomach. You don't have to worry about that."

We slowly climbed the stairs and he leaned me against the railing as he searched his wallet for the key card.

"As your doctor, I advise you to drink some water. Lots of water. That's what's good for you right now."

I was going to remind him that he was just a biology student, but it instead came out as a sort of moaning gibberish.

"What's that?" He leaned in closely. "What do you need?"

But instead of words, from my mouth and nose

shot a hearty sneeze, the kind where your chest and shoulders hurt afterward.

"Ah, that's fuckin' gross! I can't believe you just did that! Some of it got in my mouth and it tasted like barf!" Before he could fully wipe his face clean on the front of his polo shirt, I sneezed again. It wasn't as powerful as the first one, but it was more direct.

"Gimme the room key," I said, snatching it from his fingertips while he continued to clean his face of my snot. "Let's go get some water." I immediately plopped down on the closest bed and closed my eyes.

"Here, take this," Hank said, handing me two aspirins and a paper cup of water. "Are you allergic to beer now?"

"Allergic to *beer*? You poor fool." I swallowed the water and pills, then tossed the little cup back at him. "There's no such thing as beer allergies. As a doctor, you should know things like that."

"Maybe it was the food then. Are you allergic to shellfish?"

"Shellfish? Yeah, you motherfucker!"

Within seconds I was once again asleep.

Captain Cheddar, the cartoon mascot on the television commercial, proudly holds up his bowl of Cheddar Puffs cereal, and with a spoon attached to where other pirates would normally have a metal hook, he hungrily shovels in several mouthfuls of the orange powder-coated orbs. Then, in a flash of animated cinematography, a ninja dressed in all black flies in to snatch away the bowl of breakfast food before whizzing back into the tree line, never so much as spilling a single drop of milk.

"Argh," growls the angry pirate. "No one had better plunder me cheddar!" And without hesitation or concern over how a decrepit old man with one hand, one leg and one eye could ever chase down a fuckin' ninja, Captain Cheddar springs into action and

35

zooms through the trees of the Caribbean island resort with his trusty parrot gripping tightly to its owner's shoulder.

Fueled by both hunger and anger, the wronged pirate quickly catches up to the ninja, grabs him around the neck with his human hand, flings him to the ground and then proceeds to beat the dog shit out of his foe with all manners of clubs, swords and one of those big-ass cannons usually mounted to the side of a ship.

Standing over the barely breathing body of his mortal enemy, Captain Cheddar once again takes a bite of Cheddar Puffs before repeating his signature catchphrase, "Argh. No one had better plunder me cheddar."

Then the ninja twitches, and so Captain Cheddar plants the tip of his wooden leg into the thief's eye socket and applies enough pressure to cause the bastard's brains to ooze from his ear canals.

It must be Saturday morning, I thought as I clicked off the television. Why else would they be advertising things toward children?

My doctor emerged from the bathroom with a towel around his waist and a toothbrush dangling from his lips.

"What time is it?" I asked, my head still pounding from the night before.

"You've been asleep for hours. I had to get dinner from the vending machine last night and order a porno just so I could fall asleep."

"You fuckin' swine. They'll charge the porno to my credit card. I'm not paying for that."

"We'll go halves on it," he said, and I reluctantly agreed in order to drop the matter.

"I'm hungry," I mumbled. "I have a hankering for some Cheddar Puffs cereal."

"There's no way we can take the Minnow," Hank argued. "That asshole in the Jeep is probably still driving around out there looking for us. As your personal physician, I advise you to take it back to the rental agency and trade it in for something different, maybe a Mustang."

"I'm not paying for that," I protested, even after he once again suggested going halves for the damn thing. "We'll walk; I need some fresh air anyway."

We decided on lunch at the Stratosphere. It was a bit pricey, for sure, but there's no Stratosphere in either New Jersey or Louisiana and we definitely wanted a break from what we knew to be our own respective realities. It was going to be a long walk, especially in flip-flops.

Out on the sidewalk, we passed by the usual crowd of men paid to hand out fliers advertising escort services, and some guy with a pet python who let people take pictures with it free of charge. Once we strolled in front of the Mirage, however, we were greeted by a different type of nutjob altogether — Christian zealots. They spent their entire daytimes and evenings telling people that Las Vegas was the very epicenter of sin, that those who partook were on their way to hell. I only wished that were still true. We ignored them the best we could, but they were very intrusive, more so than the smut peddlers. And the damned red hand was illuminated on the sign across the corner of the street, warning us against crossing through the traffic.

"Fuck it," I said. "Let's just go. Pick up your sandals and run."

"As your doctor, I advise you not to do that. If there's one thing the cops here won't tolerate, it's jaywalking. You'll just give them an excuse to shoot."

I was about to take my chances when a young portly girl from the group approached us and asked us how we felt about Barack Obama.

"Obama? I didn't vote for that son-of-a-bitch," I said to her, still staring across the street and waiting for the little white man to take the place of the red hand.

"Did you know he wants to increase the amounts of abortions people get throughout the United States, even late term abortions, and make the taxpayers pay for it all?"

"Not my concern," I told her. "Democrats get abortions. More abortions mean less future Democrats. The problem will work itself out eventually." I cursed the traffic some more and the girl focused her attention entirely on Hank.

"Where are you guys headed?"

"To the Stratosphere to get something to eat," he

answered.

"Oh, I could really use a burger right now," she pined, though a run on a treadmill would have obviously been a wiser decision for her. "I'd have to take the buns off, though."

"Why would you take the buns off a hamburger?" my polite friend asked her.

"They're full of carbohydrates, and I'm too fat."

"Oh, you're not fat," Hank replied, forever playing the role of the nice guy, even to girls he has no intention of banging. "Why would you say that?"

"Are you kidding me?" I returned to the conversation. "Open your fuckin' eyes and look at her!"

The crowd around us drew a collective angry sigh, which signaled my time to dare the jaywalking. My flip-flops smacking quickly against the bottoms of my feet sounded something like a sick motorboat, and I didn't slow down once I hopped the opposite curb.

I stopped at a little store across the street and bought a tall can of cheap beer, sat on a bench gulping down the beverage and smoking a Marlboro. As I was finishing the beer, my cell phone rang. It was my doctor.

"Dude, where the fuck did you go?"

"I'm sitting down, probably just up the road from you. Did you lose the fatty?"

"Yeah, I got rid of her, but not before she asked me for my phone number. And of course I didn't give it to her. I gave her your number instead."

"You goddamn motherfuckin' whore!" But before I could threaten to cut him, he hung up on me and within a few seconds was approaching the bench, grinning like a retard. And then we were once again on our way to the Stratosphere.

After riding the elevator all the way up to the flying saucer perched atop a concrete stick high above the Stratosphere casino, we had trouble getting in to the restaurant. The girl behind the little counter there wasn't exactly happy that we hadn't made reservations, but there were some tables available. What she couldn't get over, however, was that we were both wearing what she called beach attire when the dress code clearly called for business casual.

"I'm self-employed," I told the snotty little bitch. "And this is what I wear to the office."

But no dice. We could not enter. After some very bad words, Hank forced a smile and asked her if we could still go outside and ride one of the crazy rollercoaster machines.

"Go ahead; there's no dress code out there," she said. "Buy the ticket, take the ride."

But I thought we *shouldn't* take the ride, and Hank agreed after I convinced him I saw a bolt or a screw or a safety pin fall off one of the rides the last time it came around. I saw no such thing, of course, but who the fuck in their right mind would climb aboard a contraption like that and allow it to toss them over the side of the fuckin' Stratosphere with only the promise that it will pull them back up safely?

Not me, by god. So we found the elevators and rode them back down nice and slowly, then hiked south again along the Strip. By the time we made it back to the Circus Circus, we were exhausted and starving.

There was definitely something wrong with a McDonald's restaurant being located inside of a historic Las Vegas casino, but hell, there was something wrong with that whole goddamn place. It was a virtual hunting ground for stoned pedophiles. They get completely ripped off of Quaaludes and drink specials at the bar, then buy the little bastard a Happy Meal and loan him a quarter for skee ball. Then, on the other side of the midway, you have grown men duking it out over who really owns the title of World's Greatest Dad, which is proudly emblazoned across the beer belly of each of their shirts.

"Let's see if there's somewhere else to eat in here," my doctor suggested. "There are many rooms in the mansion."

"No, this is fine. Let's just get a Big Mac and get the fuck outta here."

Finally, we had a chance to sit down and rest our feet a bit. Unlike Hank, I was not accustomed to traipsing around town in flip-flop sandals. I wanted to stay a while, relax, reappraise the whole situation, figure out if this town was still toxic or if the American Dream had encroached upon the one last stronghold.

Hank spotted what he determined to be a pervert

several yards down. I can only assume he hasn't had much experience with childfuckers, but I could understand Hank's reasoning there. The man, who appeared to be in his mid-fifties, was big and black, and he was escorting around a small snow-white child. The colors just didn't match, and discrepancies like that are apparently more obvious and relevant to a guy from southern Louisiana. Hank glared at the man from far away, never breaking his stare and wincing his eyes with more hate and contempt the closer the couple got to us.

"That *ain't* your boy," Hank hissed to the man as he and the kid strolled by, hand-in-hand. "We *know* that ain't your boy."

"Excuse me?" the man asked, clearly confused. "What'd you say to me?"

"We *know* what's going on here," my doctor continued. "But just tell me one thing: do you love that boy?"

Without so much as a call for explanation, the big man backhanded Hank's soda cup, exploding it and sending Coke and ice over the edge and onto the slot machines on the ground floor. He had tears welling up in his eyes and he knew the jig was up. He'd have to give up the child and find a new companion up in Carson City. Yes, sir, he was fucked.

"What's going on up here?" a man in a vest asked as he hurriedly approached us from the ramp. "Who's throwing ice?"

"These two motherfuckers just accused me of

stealing my grandchild," the angry black man roared. "This here's my grandson, his mama's down the way, and these two motherfuckers are accusing me of stealing him. Why, because I'm black? You two in the Klan, motherfuckers? I want the police here right now! I'm gonna sue the shit outta this place!"

"Wanda, call the police," the vested man called out to one of his subordinates. "Sir, we're gonna take care of this right here. The police will be here soon to straighten it all out, and in the meantime, we should all just lower our voices and watch our language as this is a family establishment."

"Unray out the oorday," my doctor mumbled to me under his breath.

"Huh?"

"It's that pig language," he clarified. "Run out the door."

And so we ran, our sandals clapping against our heels, all the way down the twisted ramp and out the front doors. We didn't let up until we hit Treasure Island.

I had expected, as I always do, that our trip would eventually involve law enforcement officials, but I had no idea it would be for inciting a race riot inside an amusement park.

"Geez," Hank sighed. "You try to help someone, and this is what it gets you. It just doesn't pay to be a nice guy anymore."

The screen to my laptop slammed down hard, assisted by my doctor's heavy hand, and my eyelids snapped immediately open, the evening's eye-boogers solidified in my eyelashes and blurring my vision

"Goddamn you," Hank scolded me. "I left you alone all night and you got nothing done!"

What time was it? Was it tomorrow already? With the curtains closed, it's hard to tell the difference between the neon glow of the street and actual sunlight. Hank flipped on the TV, and I could tell by the content that I had not slept into morning.

Two police officers wait patiently in their patrol car, which is partially hidden behind a billboard on the side of a two-lane highway. A shiny silver luxury

44

car cruises toward the officers and the driver, a black man in his mid-thirties wearing a nice suit, reaches into the briefcase on his front passenger seat and retrieves a granola bar. He takes a bite from the bar just as he passes by the police car.

The police officers, both young white guys, flip on the lights and siren and give chase until their suspect pulls his car to the side of the road.

"Is there a problem, officers?" the worried driver asks the approaching cops. "Was I speeding?"

"Sir, we're the Breakfast Police, and that granola bar there puts you in serious violation."

One of the cops opens the man's door and motions for him to step out, then hands him an already poured bowl of cereal.

"You see, sir, Cheddar Puffs cereal has all the vitamins, minerals and nutrients you just won't get from a granola bar. Plus, it's coated in a delicious cheese-flavored powder."

After devouring the cereal, the man gulps down the rest of the milk in the bowl.

"Mmm, cheese milk!" he smiles, as an orange milk mustache is revealed.

"We don't wanna see you out here violating the laws of a healthy breakfast anymore, you hear?" the other cops warns. "Now, assume the position."

The perpetrator smiles, then places both hands on the hood of the police car. The commercial ends with the Breakfast Police beating the black man bloody with their billy clubs.

It was still evening. I stood up as empty beer cans fell all around me on the floor. I found a puddle of drool had formed under my head on the table.

"Am I not considerate?" Hank asked me. "Did I not let you sleep? And if you did wake up, did I not give you a free show? And you couldn't even have the decency to save me one fuckin' beer?"

"What the fuck are you talking about, you fuckin' swine?"

"Man, you really were out like a light, weren't you. I thought you were just faking, but you really were passed the fuck out?"

I didn't say a word, but my confused look must've begged further explanation.

"Here," he began, "I want you to have all the background." He cleared his throat and prepared himself for a tale of historic magnitude. "You see, I left here earlier, approximately five hours ago, and drove myself, alone, to the Denny's up the Strip. I had one of those bacon avocado burritos, which was on time, by the way. And I met there a young girl who was clearing dirty dishes off the tables. We'll just call her Nancy."

"What was her real name?"

"Nancy," he repeated. "She was a female busboy, Mexican-style, and she barely spoke a word of English. To make a long story short, she asked me for a ride home, I agreed, and twenty minutes later we were in the back seat of the Minnow, stuffed in like a can of sardines and making stains on the upholstery."

"You asshole! You're gonna pay for those stains. They're gonna charge that to my credit card."

"We'll go halves," my doctor told me before continuing his story. "Well, the back seat of the Minnow was too small and Nancy kept making all sorts of Spanish noises when she hit her head against the glass, and that attracted the attention of the folks

46

going into the Denny's. So I told her we had to go back to her place. But no dice; she still lives with her parents. So I brought her here, and we hammered out our details right there on your bed."

"On my bed? You dirty motherfucker!"

"It was closer. And when I was all done, I told her to get dressed so I could drive her home." Hank paused, then stared me directly in the eyes for emphasis. "She had me drop her off at a van in the Wal-Mart parking lot. Isn't that just the craziest thing you've ever heard? Oh, and I gave her your cell phone number, just in case she wanted to call me."

"Give those bitches your own number next time," I instructed him as I pulled a drivers license out from under a corner of the bed sheet. "It's Nancy's ID. Damn, she's only eighteen-years-old?"

"Eighteen? Is that what it says? She looks more like fifteen in person."

My cell phone began vibrating in my pocket and upon retrieving it I noticed I had a few missed calls and two unheard voice messages.

The first message was from the fat anti-abortion girl Hank had befriended earlier in the afternoon. She said her name was Melanie, which made sense because she resembled a melon, and she was clearly stuffing her face as she grunted into the telephone. I could hear the grease dripping from her lips and onto the phone receiver, and then she licked it off before continuing the message. She wanted Hank, and she was hungry.

"Just delete that one," Hank instructed me. "And if you ever talk to that poor girl again, I want you to let her down easy for me."

It took half a roll of duct tape, but the passenger side mirror was once again attached to the car door.

"Where's the real Vegas at?" my doctor asked. "We came here to get away from average America, but instead we're caught right in the fuckin' vortex. This is the Disneyland of the goddamn desert. A fuckin' Vegas-themed family playground."

"You wanna go back to Fremont Street? We can see if that old woman and her friends are there."

"No, but I have an idea." Then he puffed up his chest and put his hands on his waist as if listening to his own theme music playing in his head. "You remember those signs they put up on the east end of Fremont? Those old signs from back in the old days? They have an outdoor museum called the Boneyard

48

that's just full of those old signs. I saw it in a magazine someplace. They're fixin' them up, putting the light bulbs back in. That place just has to be authentic Vegas."

So we asked for directions from a homeless guy at the gas station and finally found the place out past the north end near Cashman Field. The place was deserted except for a young couple with professional-looking cameras and a laptop computer, which one of them typed away on as I pulled the car up next to them. When I asked them if it was indeed the museum, the one on the laptop told me the place was closed to the general public and tours were only available with a scheduled appointment. None of us would be getting in without breaking and entering, and the photographers seemed almost willing to go that route.

"What now?" I asked. "Sunbathing poolside at the Mirage?"

"It's the middle of the goddamn night. Besides, they won't let us near the pool without paying for a room first."

"MGM?"

"Yuma."

"Yuma?" We spent our time stationed in Yuma waiting for the weekends so that we could drive to Las Vegas, and now Hank was actually suggesting that we leave Las Vegas to visit Yuma?

"Yuma," my doctor repeated. "At least we know that place is decrepit, uncompromised by yuppies searching for the American Dream. If a thing like this is worth doing at all, it's worth doing right."

We were once again headed south along the Strip, hoping we could remember the way back to the bottom of Arizona and knowing that there were actually very few roadways involved. But I was hungry, so we stopped at a little Chinese place at the end of town while I confirmed driving directions with the Internet on my cell phone.

"Welcome here," an Asian gentleman smiled as we entered the Golden Dragon. "Two you?"

"No, I'm not eating," Hank explained to the man. "I already had a burrito at Denny's."

"You order, you eat," the man replied. "You eat, you pay."

"But I'm not hungry. I've already eaten."

"Is buffet," the man insisted. "You order, you eat. You eat, you pay. Two you?"

"Yes," I interrupted, trying to avoid an argument. "Two of us."

The restaurant was small, and we brought our plates of fried rice and eggrolls to an empty booth. At the next booth over was an older man with wiry grey hair and a green military-style jacket. In addition to the wearing of a heavy coat in Las Vegas in the middle of summer, this man came off as possibly crazy for other reasons, as well. For example, he ate his rice with a fork that folded out from an oversized Swiss Army Knife and talked to himself on a pair of portable radios.

"Raven leader, this is the colonel. Can you hear me, son?" He spoke into one radio while holding the other one up to his ear, then switched their positions before responding. "Yes, colonel, I hear you. I'm awaiting your orders, sir."

I leaned across the table toward Hank and whispered quietly, "Don't say a word. Just eat your food so we can get out of here."

Unfortunately, we didn't eat quickly enough because the crazy guy pocketed his knife, then stood and approached our table with the two radios in hand. We tried to ignore him, hoping he'd simply walk out the door and be gone from the parking lot before it was our turn to leave. But there he was, standing at the edge of our table, sizing us up as we avoided eye contact and finished our meals.

"Here," the man said, handing one of the radios to Hank. "I'm gonna go out into the parking lot and you're gonna stay right here. I need to make sure these things will work with some distance between them."

Hank accepted the radio and the man bolted for the door. My doctor and I watched the man through the window as he jogged to the far corner of the small parking lot and tested the devices.

"Raven leader, this is the colonel. Can you hear me?"

"Colonel, this is the raven leader," Hank responded cautiously. "I hear you loud and clear."

"Good, son. You just wait right there. I'll be right back." The colonel climbed into a small car and squealed the tires as he ripped out of the parking lot. After several seconds, he broke radio silence. "You still hear me, boy?"

We wanted to run. But where would we go? This man could easily hunt us down like dogs and carve us up with his pocketknife.

"There's plenty of vultures out here," my doctor informed me. "They'll pick our bones clean before morning."

Yes, the best thing to do in a situation like that is to simply stay put. There were witnesses inside. They could be useful in helping the police identify our bodies. When we saw the colonel's car return to the parking lot, I told Hank I needed to piss and I scrambled to the restroom. With any luck, I thought, he'd be gone before I came back. At the very worst, the colonel would murder everyone there, but at least I'd be protected by the slide bolt lock on the restroom door. But when I got back, the colonel was in my seat, yapping it up with my friend.

"So I hear you boys are military," the old man said as I approached the table.

"Former military," I corrected him, but I don't think he heard me.

"Sergeant Matthews here says you're on board to join my outfit. What's your name, son?"

"Victor," I said, snapping to attention and whipping up my hand to salute. "Corporal Zulu, actually. What's the battle plan, sir? Are we robbing a casino?"

"Just keep your voice down, Danny Ocean," the colonel hushed me. "And you ain't no corporal, neither. We've got a rank structure here. You're Private Third Class Zulu, and you report to Sergeant Matthews here. And Sergeant Matthews reports directly to me."

"And who do you report to, sir?"

The colonel gave me the stank eye and leaned in close. "You ask too many questions. As far as you're concerned, I'm the H.M.F.I.C. — the Head Motherfucker In Charge." He handed Hank one of the radios, told him to rally his troops and muster at the convoy outside. With that, the colonel was once again sprinting through the Golden Dragon and out the door to his car. We followed slowly.

"What the fuck have you gotten us into?" I asked Hank as we climbed into the Minnow. "Fuck him. Let's just take off and pawn the radio. How much do you think we can get for it?"

"Raven leader, this is the colonel. I'm in the black Acura with the twenty-inch rims. You stay on my bumper, and don't you boys even think aborting the mission and running away with my radio or I'll try you for treason and handle the sentencing myself."

"Should we follow him?" I asked. "The guy is obviously crazy."

"But that's why we're here, to find the edge of madness and stop just short of going over. He'll take us there, and we'll watch him go over."

"Yeah, but he might take us with him."

I tailgated the colonel all the way out of town, out past the last-chance gas stations and the rundown strip clubs that were probably also brothels. I no longer even knew which direction we were heading and hoped nothing would obscure our view of the light atop the Luxor. It's bright enough to guide you home from the moon if you need it to, just so long as you're still able to see that side of the world.

We left the main roads far behind us; the Strip wasn't even within walking distance anymore. We putted along back roads I never even knew existed outside Vegas and I remember being amazed by the number of little hills discreetly hidden away in plain sight around that part of the desert. Immediately following a sharp left turn, the black Acura ahead of us finally pulled over to the side of the road in the middle of absolutely nowhere, and so did we. Once I shut off the engine, the colonel exited his vehicle and started back to meet us.

"This is the part where he shoots us and steals the Minnow," I feared aloud.

"Dude drives a brand new Acura," Hank reminded me. "Why would he want a Nissan Versa?"

Just the same, a fear crept up on the both of us and gyrated through our bodies like a severe case of the piss shivers. The colonel tapped on Hank's window with the radio and instructed us to get out of the car. I hesitated and slid the key back into the ignition.

"If you start the car now," my doctor warned, "he'll shoot us both before you even get it into gear."

And he was right. The colonel had obviously seen some serious shit in his day, and I did not want to be remembered in one of his future flashbacks. The old man motioned for us to follow him on foot up the road, and so we went. We all stopped at the top of a small hill, about a hundred yards from where we left the cars, and looked out into the darkness that was broken only by the four-way flashing red light at an intersection just beyond the other side of the hill.

"That's where you boys will be situated," the colonel said, pointing down to the crossroads below the red glow. "You gotta watch out for any traffic. I'm gonna start back there where the car is now, rev it up and fly in this direction. If you see anybody coming from any direction, you call me on the radio."

"Understood," Sergeant Matthews said, though I could see in his eyes that he was just as confused as I was.

"But don't you boys stand in the way there, or I'll land right on top of you. If it wasn't for that damned cross street I could do it all by myself. And if it wasn't for that hairpin turn going the other way there, I'd just jump it in that direction. That's how we tried it the last time, when Sergeant Lawson was driving. He's dead now. I don't like it when my men die on me."

And then all was silent as the colonel's eyes focused on something far off in the distance, possibly from another time altogether. A flashback, maybe? I was just glad he was driving the car this time instead of delegating the task to one of us. I didn't know who the hell Sergeant Lawson was, but I began to feel as though his ghost was standing there with us, urging us to run into the darkness and not look back. After all, the crazy fucker couldn't shoot what he couldn't see.

"Have you ever killed a man?" the colonel inquired of me, his eyes now looking through my own and into my mind itself.

"No, but one time I killed a rat with a stick."

"You think you're pretty funny, don't you, Private Fourth Class Zulu." I'd apparently just been demoted one rank. "But you don't know what funny is. Funny is putting a dead Iraqi in the front seat of a Toyota Corolla and taking pictures with him. Now *that's* funny." Then he studied us silently with a deep, penetrating stare. "You'll kill somebody one day, and it'll change your life, so be ready for it. Now you two get your fuckin' asses down that hill and watch for traffic."

We did as we were told, not because we were loyal to our commanding officer, but because we greatly feared him. We hiked to our assigned positions as he went back down the other side of the hill.

"I hope he just takes the Minnow and leaves," I said. "I'd rather answer to the car rental people than to be gutted by this psychopath. Plus, we could blame him for the broken mirror."

After a couple of minutes, we could hear the Acura rev up its engine on the other side of the hill.

"How's it looking over there, boys?" The colonel was ready to go.

Hank looked each way before answering, "All clear, sir."

The Acura revved up a few more times, and then we heard it drive away. With any luck, I thought, he had hooked up a towrope to the Nissan and was leaving us stranded. The temperatures at night there were bearable. By the time we got dehydrated, we'd be back in civilization. We've both run marathons before; a leisurely walk shouldn't be a problem.

A pair of headlights appeared in the distance on the cross street, and they got bigger and brighter over the next few seconds.

"Put your thumb in the air," I told Hank. "We'll ask these folks for a ride into town. And show some fuckin' leg, you pansy."

About the time the vehicle was close enough to be recognized as a police cruiser, the colonel was once again on speaking terms with us.

"Alright, boys, I'm past the point of no return. I'll be seeing you soon!"

We turned to walk back toward the hill while Hank radioed the colonel. "Stop the car, sir. Abort, I repeat, abort! There's a fuckin' cop over here." But there was no answer. The mastermind had either left us there to deal with the police, or he couldn't hear the last transmission over the scream of the engine.

The policeman turned on his flashing lights as he passed by us walking back toward the hill, then he made a quick U-turn and slowed his car to a stop next to us on the side of the road. "Stop," he directed us via the cruiser's PA system. We did as we were told, and he stepped out of his vehicle with his right hand at his holster.

"What's that you got there?" he asked, ready to draw down and shoot from the hip at our first questionable move.

"It's just a radio," Hank told him. "A walkie-talkie."

"What the hell do you need a walkie-talkie out here for? Just what the hell are you *doing* here?"

The sound of the speeding Acura was once again present, though only a low hum somewhere off in the distance, probably unnoticeable except to someone listening attentively for it specifically. This is great, I thought. The colonel could come and explain to the cop the plan better than we ever could, and we could be on our way. There's no chance the old man would dare shoot us with a police officer present. At the very least, if something illegal is happening, Hank and I were nothing more than simple patsies. We were just holding a radio, and that's certainly not a crime.

"We're waiting for a ride," I told the cop. "He should be here any minute."

"Well, you'd better hope so." And then he squinted as he studied us harder. "You guys doing drugs out here? Are you waiting on your drug dealer?"

"No, we're waiting on our ride," Hank reiterated to the cop. "I think I hear him coming."

"Well, he'd better get here soon, or else you two fellas look mighty suspicious standing out here in the middle of nowhere, with no car and just that goddamn walkie-talkie."

And with a roar of his tiny Japanese car's engine, the colonel was finally there. We could hear the car up close — hell, we could smell the fuckin' thing — long before we ever saw so much as the headlights, which were pointed straight to the heavens as the Acura cleared the top of the hill and flew just above our heads before slamming hard onto the street maybe twelve feet from where we stood. All four wheels buckled under, and the vehicle slid on its undercarriage, sparks flying every which way and the weight of the ride digging long black grooves into surface of the street.

"Hot damn!" yelled the cop as he began his foot chase of the stunt vehicle. "You two stay right there."

When the Acura finally came to a rest just past the intersection with the blinking red light, the driver door flew open and the colonel stepped out, removing what appeared to be an old World War II-era combat helmet from his skull, tossing it to the pavement and throwing his arms in the air in apparent victory.

"Woo!" the colonel screamed into the air before his sight focused on the cop closing in on him, his gun drawn and sighted in. "Better run, boys! I'll meet back up with you at the rendezvous."

And so we ran, back up the hill and to the Minnow. Then we tore out of there without hesitation or any clear idea of where we really were. Finally, we saw the Luxor's beam and we aimed ourselves at it.

We spent the rest of that night drinking at the Riviera, smoking cigarettes and feeding dollar bills into the video poker machines on top of the bar until the sun came up. My doctor, always the sensitive one, was showing signs of worry, or at least wonder.

"Colonel, can you hear me?" he spoke into the portable radio. "This is the raven leader." But there was no answer. The colonel was probably in jail, forcefully sodomized by a gang of street hoodlums picked up for spray painting their names on some old building in the north side. Or he was in a mental facility under close observation, which was actually more likely. "Raven leader to the colonel. Can you hear me, sir?"

"Yes, raven leader, I hear you." But it was obviously not the colonel's voice. "Report your twenty and I'll make rendezvous with you there."

59

"They've got him," I said, "and now they're coming after us."

"They'll never find us if we don't tell them where we are."

"Goddamn you, man, you're not thinking," I told him. "These things have electronic tracking devices built in, like GPS. They're probably on their way here now."

I slapped a ten-dollar bill on the bar and instructed the bartender to tell no one we'd been there, and then we made our exit.

"Toss that radio in the trash," I told Hank. "It's covered in our prints."

"Well, we're fucked now," my doctor assessed. "Probably every cop in Clark County is out looking for us. And here we are, sticking out like a sore thumb in this candy apple-red buggy."

"It's a common car," I told him, pointing out two more identical vehicles on the Strip. "All we have to do is drive around town and knock the right side-view mirror off of every red Nissan Versa we see. They'll never be able to tell us apart."

"You're an idiot," hank said. "We have to get outta town."

But where would we go? Yuma, we decided, was a bad decision. We could drive four hours straight, but for what? Decent Mexican food? The cops probably had a roadblock on every road out of town. Besides, there was a Del Taco just up the road. But now was no time for eating. We were on the lam.

"We need some place to hide out," I resolved.

"Billie Jo?"

"Ah, yes. Billie Jo."

My doctor had known Billie Jo for several years, at least a decade, ever since he was first stationed in Arizona. A Marine he had worked with was a Las Vegas native who brought Hank up a few times and introduced him to the beautiful Billie Jo.

Hank was immediately infatuated with her and it broke his heart when an actual relationship never fully materialized between them. She got married, but Hank still pined for Billie Jo. Then Hank got married, and he still pined for Billie Jo, but he did so quietly. Even after she had a few kids, he was still fascinated with this "one who got away." They still kept in contact through occasional emails and such, but that was about it.

But now things have changed. He was recently divorced and in town, and he once again wanted to know, for his own records, whether he could have ever had a chance with her if the distance between them had not been a factor.

I steered the Minnow onto the freeway, as per my doctor's advice, and got off on a more quiet and secluded stretch of road which eventually led us up the drive of a high-class country club.

"Does she still work here?" I asked Hank, who shrugged off the question. "Well, then, let's go find out."

We found a place to park and trekked up to what we figured was the main entrance. There was a girl behind the counter there, but she was not Billie Jo. Hank asked her if his old friend was working that day, but the girl seemed unsure.

"Billie?" she asked. "I'm not sure who that is, but I'm also pretty new here. Is she a blonde?"

"Sometimes," Hank answered.

"Well, if she is working today, she's probably on her lunch break. You might wanna try back in maybe an hour or so."

I didn't feel like having to leave just to come back again, so I asked the nice young girl if we could tour the golf course, inspect the putting greens.

"Are you thinking of becoming members?" she asked.

"Well, now that'll just depend on if we find your putting greens to be satisfactory enough."

She copied our information from our driver's licenses and gave us grounds passes. Then we set off to stretch our legs and kill some time.

Hank was down, not the upbeat and adventurous animal he had been the night before, when he first got us into this mess. I could see the depression forming in the areas just beyond the glossy portion of his eyeballs.

"The bottom of my foot feels crazy," he said.

"What the hell does that mean?"

"I don't know," he answered. "It's just how I feel."

And I knew exactly how he felt. I didn't feel the same way, of course, as collateral damage is always present when Hank and I run rampant. I accepted it, though Hank usually tried to avoid it. The *it* this time, specifically, was an elderly man in a green pickup truck who impeded our escape from law enforcement the night before. We scared him, I was sure of that much, but the extent of his mental injury was still unclear. Could he still function in a regular society afterward? Will he ever step foot out of his home again?

Hank has always been prone to road rage, but probably no more than the average American driver. I, on the other hand, go absolutely fuckin' ballistic when behind the wheel and sharing the streets with morons. So it's a good thing I wasn't driving the night before, I figured, or else we all might have died.

Hank, being more experienced than most others in sprinting in sandals, made it back to the car before me and jumped in the driver seat. By the time I had made it down the hill, the Minnow was already idling and in gear. I had to jump in as Hank executed a quick U-turn and sped away from the crime scene, from the colonel and the cop, with the headlights off to avoid detection.

It wasn't but a few miles and a couple of direction changes down the road before our path was obscured by an old green truck, weaving ever so slightly back and forth across both lanes of the desolate stretch of blacktop.

"Just pass the sonofabitch," I commanded, but there was no way around. Was the driver drunk, or maybe visually impaired? Either way, he was in our way. "Flip on the headlights. Maybe he doesn't know someone is behind him."

The lights seemed to confuse the driver more, and we were sure he was heavily intoxicated. Hank laid on the horn, but it made no difference. Once the truck weaved far enough into the right shoulder, Hank gunned it to the left, but was cut off by the returning green truck. For a moment there, it looked as though the guy was just fucking with us, content with going twenty miles-per-hour below the speed limit and unwilling to let anybody else pass. Hank rode the truck's bumper, and at the next opportunity, he once again jumped on the gas pedal.

As we passed the truck, the driver peered at me through thick-framed spectacles. He was about a hundred and fifteen years old and he had his face shoved as far forward as it could physically get, a desperate attempt at a better view of the road beyond midnight. Though I had been expecting a drunk bastard to flip me the finger while we passed, who I was instead faced against was somebody's great-grandfather, probably older than Las Vegas itself, and clearly too old to be driving alone after dark.

But that was no excuse, and so as we passed, I rolled down my window and climbed halfway out of the car, holding myself in with my left hand and waving my right fist at the geriatric bastard, screaming, "Get the fuck outta the way, you old motherfucker!"

That seemed to do the trick. The green truck quickly slowed down and came to a complete stop in the middle of the road.

"Serves him right," I said, glancing back through the duct tape-covered mirror. "Now, if the cops are still chasing us, he should slow them down a bit."

"He was just an old man," my doctor whined from the middle of the golf course. "You can't fuck with old people like that. They're fragile."

"He was standing between us and freedom," I explained to my accomplice. "You think Bonnie and Clyde would've let something like that happen? No, they would've shot him right in the face, and all we did was honk and yell."

"We're not Bonnie and Clyde."

"You got that right, buddy. You'd be one ugly fuckin' Bonnie."

Hank got that demon look in his eyes again and I thought he was going to hit me, but he instead grabbed my head and shoved me to the left. "Look out!" he said, just as a small white orb flew past the both of us. We looked back, far behind, and saw four golfers at two golf carts.

"Move. Your. Ass!" one man yelled at us, very slowly and methodically to ensure he was understood. "We're. Playing. Through!"

"I can't believe that sonofabitch tried to hit us," I said. "He did that on purpose."

My doctor was less concerned with possible death and instead fixed his attention on one of the golfers.

"Is that Alice Cooper?" he asked me, pointing at the group. "I think that's Alice Cooper."

"Alice Cooper? No, I think that's a woman."

"That's just what Alice Cooper would *want* you to think," Hank reasoned before yelling out toward the group. "Are you Alice Cooper?"

"Go for it," one of the other golfers said to the man with the long black hair before placing a ball on a tee for his friend.

That longhaired man — quite possibly the veteran rock star — got into his stance, performed a comical waggle, back swung and then shot. The ball went high and I was blinded as it flew into the sun, and then the ball was gone. Vanished. But the golfers were still staring at us, waiting.

And when it finally touched down, it sent Hank back hard, hunched over in the fetal position and unable to breathe. Right in the fuckin' gut.

"Ah can't breave," Hank whispered, grasping for breath. "He kilt me."

Over the laughter of the asshole golfers, I rolled my doctor onto his back and pulled his yellow polo shirt up to expose his belly, which was bright red except for the massive purple welt at the place of impact.

"Hematoma, motherfucker!" he screamed, curling back up into a cannonball. "Massive subcutaneous ecchymosis as a result of blunt force trauma to the abdomen. I think it ruptured my fuckin' spleen."

"Easy there, weirdo," I tried to calm him. "You aren't even a real doctor, so shut your goddamn mouth!"

"Take me home to Louisiana. Don't let me die out here in the desert."

Not a chance. If there's one thing I've learned throughout my life, it's that you never leave a friend behind, no matter how crippled and worthless he may have just become. But first, I had a few choice words for the attacker.

"Are you really Alice Cooper?" I yelled, but that only made them laugh more.

I told my buddy to relax, to not worry about a thing, and then I took him by the ankles and dragged him through the grass, all the way to the parking lot. He was in no condition to see Billie Jo, and I was in no mood for another attack by a fuckin' psychopath, Alice Cooper or not.

Hank was awake again when we pulled into the hotel parking lot, so I let him walk himself up the stairs. The desk woman was out front enjoying her cigarette and my doctor had already given her weird vibes during previous encounters. If I carried him up the stairs now fireman-style, that would only arouse her suspicion.

My doctor isn't like normal people; he's different, a true one-of-a-kind — and for very good reason. If everyone else thought like him, the world would be a much more fucked-up place. For starters, all clothing would carry the Lacoste crocodile. That alone is too much for decent people to handle.

I went up the steps ahead of him. If that big bastard went down, the last place I wanted to be was under him. Catching him be damned; just let him fall and stay out of the way. Luckily, he made it to the room without incident.

"You need to relax," I told him. "Sit down. I'll find something on the television." But when I turned it on, there was only an infomercial starring some woman in a navy blue pantsuit.

Hotel televisions are useless in Las Vegas. There's nothing good on for free. Trying to keep you in the room is pointless. Why curl up on the bed with a sitcom when there's money to be spent outside? If you really want to watch the tube, you'll either pay for the premium channels or suffer through infomercials. Pretty serious shit, too.

"Hello," says the woman in the pantsuit, "I'm here to talk to you about something affecting seventy-five percent of school-age children. It's called depression, and it's very real. Teen suicides are on the rise all over the nation, but your child doesn't need to be a victim. That's why there's Cheddar Puffs brand breakfast cereal. It gives children the vitamins and nutrients they need, and with the orange cheese-flavored powder coating they crave. After one bite of Cheddar Puffs, your child will realize that life really is worth living, and maybe he'll think twice about hanging himself in the closet with a belt."

"Turn that shit off," Hank was moaning from his bed. "Put on the Wallflowers. I need something for my headache. You got any medicine?"

I pointed to the bathroom as I continued to dig through my suitcase, eventually producing the CD he had requested. Hank went through my hygiene bag, desperate for a cure for what ailed him.

"How many should I take?" he asked after locating my medicine stash.

"Just a couple."

"Well, alright then," he replied as he rattled some pills from a bottle, tossed them down his neck and washed them down with a glass of tap water. "Lexapro, Wellbutrin, what is this?"

"I got it from some quack doctor. He said it's used to fix people's heads when their brains get broken. Don't worry; it's absolutely pure. You'd better lie down."

I turned on the Wallflowers CD, set it on repeat and cranked it up loud so he could fall asleep easier. That headache medicine could sometimes cause insomnia, so I knew that his getting some decent rest was paramount. "Can I get you anything?"

He waved me away, so I decided to give him some time to recuperate from the attack. I told him I was going out for quesadillas, maybe to look for some breakfast cereal, and then I shut the door behind me.

It had been a rough few days and I needed to recharge, but I knew it best to stay conservative. So I ordered six quesadillas and a medium Coke. I also requested a stopwatch, but that only caused confusion at the counter.

About the time I was swallowing down my second Del Taco delicacy, that rotund Melanie plowed through the door, almost taking it off the hinges. She plopped down across the table from me so hard I had to question the integrity of the chair's construction. Amazingly, it withstood.

"Pretty fuckin' sturdy," I said, leaning over to check out the chair legs. "Not even bowing. Must be reinforced steel."

"I'm up here, Romeo," she smiled, and so I returned to my meal. "Where's Hank? Is he taking a pee or something?"

"No, he's sick," I explained, though I thought about letting her into our hotel room to have her way with him so that I could photograph the look on his face as he wakes up and becomes aware that he's the victim of some kind of interspecies rape. No, I thought, that's probably not a good idea. Depression is a serious illness and waking up to this bovine might only worsen his symptoms. "It's probably best to just let him sleep a while."

"Well, darn it all," she moped. "Because I was just driving by this place on my way to get a salad or something healthy, and I saw you walking in here. I figured Hank must've been with you, so I turned around. And now I guess I'll just have to eat here, even though it ain't right for my diet."

"You really don't have to tell me this stuff." I started stuffing entire quesadillas into my mouth. I needed to get out of there, and quickly.

"I was on that Atkins Diet for a while, and then I tried being a vegetarian for about six months, and then I tried these pills that cut the fat out of your food."

"I really don't care."

"Yeah, but those pills were more of an inconvenience than anything else. They caused some greasy anal leakage, and combined with my collapsible butthole, it was a lot to worry about. You know what I mean? Think about all the nutrients lost. But it'll all be worth it once I slim down to under two hundred pounds. But even that will be just the beginning of my transformation."

"Alright then, you crazy bitch, I have to go." I stood up, slid my uneaten food and beverage into the trashcan and flung my tray up on top. "Look, I don't mean to be rude, but I have to leave. I think I may have the swine flu, and you need to just stay the fuck away from me."

"Okay," she smiled. "Tell Hank I hope he's feeling better."

"Get back in your cage, weirdo."

I figured that by the time I got back, my doctor might be awake and rejuvenated, but probably still down. There's only one real cure for depression, temporary or otherwise, and Hank was my friend. So, on my way back to the hotel, I stopped at a liquor store and picked up a bottle of Jack Daniel's Single Barrel. And since I was feeling older than my age would suggest, I also bought a two-liter of Coke for a chaser, some plastic cups and a bag of ice.

When I opened the door of the hotel room, Hank was still passed out, and the Wallflowers music was still blaring at nearly full volume. I didn't want to drink alone, but I also knew the risks involved with waking a supposedly sane man under the influence of illegally obtained mind-altering prescription drugs. So I pulled the chair out to the balcony, scooped some ice into a cup and poured some Jack over it.

The ice was no match for the desert heat, so the bourbon was watered down just enough to give the beverage a more mellow, sweeter flavor. After a while, I didn't even bother with the ice, and I never opened the Coke.

I woke up to the cleaning lady pushing my legs off the railing with her vacuum cleaner, mumbling something in what I assumed was Spanish. Scattered around me on the balcony were a whole pack's worth of cigarette butts and an empty bottle of Jack Daniel's Single Barrel. The sun scorching my face told me it was morning, but my pounding migraine said I needed more sleep. The hangover, however, wasn't quite as bad as I had expected it to be.

As I stood and collected myself, a giant predatory bird of some kind made its presence known with a shrill but quiet squawk, apparently disappointed in my movement.

"I ain't dead yet, you bastard," I said to it as I opened the door to the room. "Come back later."

Hank was not in his bed, which somewhat startled me, but I could hear the sink running in the

72

bathroom and his razor clanking against the side of the sink. All was normal, I thought, until I heard what may have been crying, or at least a mournful groaning, as he washed off the agony he had accumulated upon himself over the past few days and tried to make himself presentable to the world again. *Ignore the terror in the bathroom,* I told myself. *He'll need some breakfast, but then he'll be okay.*

Hank finally emerged from the steamy bathroom with a towel around his waist just as I pushed the play button on the portable CD player to once again blast the music from our lone album.

"Turn that shit off!" my doctor demanded. "What the fuck did you give me last night? That medicine almost killed me."

"Which bottle did you get it from?"

"I don't know. One of your medicine bottles. I thought it was Motrin, but it gave me the chills and had me tossing all night. I've had a fever and stomach aches and that goddamn Wallflowers, all night long, just made it worse. If I hear that song again, I'll fuckin' kill somebody."

"No, man, that wasn't Motrin. You took something better. How's the stomach now?"

"I woke up this morning when the maid came in to tidy up, but I told her we'd clean the room ourselves," he explained. "She said she thought you were dead outside and wanted to know if I'd like a newspaper. But I couldn't tell her no in Spanish, so I told her I'd take one if she'd just close the fuckin' door and never come back."

"How much did the paper cost? They'll charge that to my card, you know."

"We'll go halves," he said before continuing. "So I took the paper to the toilet so I could read the comics. That medicine you gave me really messed up my bowels so bad that I devastated the commode bowl, made a real mess of things. It blasted out from the toilet and completely ruined the funny pages. If I even tried to wipe, I would've had to start way up here on the back of my neck."

"Holy shit!" I winced at his description.

"So I did the only thing I could do. I flushed the comics and climbed into the shower. It was the *only* way. And when I stepped out of the shower, I looked down and I was standing on a story in the paper that you might find interesting."

He retrieved the soggy paper, opened up to a few pages in, and pointed out the article.

Per the newspaper story, the local cops had been called out to a possible homicide in the middle of some backstreet after a passerby found a dead man on the side of the road. Initially thought to be a carjacking or robbery gone wrong, Ernesto Sandoval, who was a member of a prominent pioneering Las Vegas family, was found slouched over in his vehicle, stone cold dead. No wounds were found on his body and it was eventually determined that he died of an apparent heart attack.

"So, what's this have to do with me?" I asked. "I like Vegas, but I never met this man. He's no kin to me. Old people die all the time. If he wasn't part of some pioneer family, it never would've made it to the newspaper. Let's go get some pancakes."

"No, you asshole, don't you get it? That's the road we were on with the colonel."

"You don't know what the hell you're talking about. You don't know street names. Why don't you just calm down and take another hit from the medicine bottle?"

"The old man in the truck. Remember?" Now he was just making to sense at all. "You yelled at him, he had a heart attack, and it killed him. You killed that man, and I'm your accomplishment."

"My *accomplice*," I corrected him. "And if anything, you're the killer and I'm your accomplice, after the fact."

"I just drove the getaway car," he insisted.

"Look, I know what you need," I said, trying to calm my almost hysterical friend. "Chinese food. It's what's good for you right now. We'll go back and find that Golden Dragon, have some eggrolls, clear our heads." I handed him the unopened bottle of warm Coke, and he unscrewed the cap and took a sip.

"Alright," he agreed. "I do need some food, but not the Golden Dragon. We need to watch out for the colonel, just in case he escaped."

"I think we've jumped the shark here," Hank said while we sat in the Minnow in the middle of a Kmart parking lot. We had spent the day feeding money into slot machines, and now we were just bored. "Anything we do now just won't make any sense. It won't add to the story. Maybe we should just cut this trip short and go home now."

"Are you kidding me? Your plane ticket's already paid for. We've got a few more days here to make this trip worthwhile."

"We may have killed a guy, for fuck's sake, and now I can't sleep."

"Just have another shot," I recommended. "A dollop'll do ya."

Hank filled his mouth with whipped cream from a can, sprinkled mini M&M's on top of the protruding mound of white fluff, and then washed it all down with eggnog that we were sure should have been pulled from the store shelves months earlier. He passed me the mixings and I took my own shot, struggling to find some sort of overused metaphor that he might actually understand to bring him around.

"You know when you're in bed and you're finally comfortable and warm and then you're too warm?" I began. "And then you move over just slightly and find a cool spot in the sheets?"

"What the fuck are you talking about, you nincomshit?" The metaphor was over his head, I guess. "I don't need a fuckin' nap, you gaywad, I need to make right with the dead guy."

"You can't make right with a dead guy, even if you did kill him. And there's no telling if he's the same guy. Unless we break into the morgue. You wanna break into the morgue?" I was up for anything at that point. A Kmart parking lot isn't always as exciting as one might hope.

"No, I'm done breaking the law. We'll just have to go to his funeral and check out the body. I saw his face. I can recognize him."

"Fuck that. You're off your rocker. I'm tired of this shit. You wanna worry yourself to death? That man was old; it was just his time. That ain't how I'm gonna go."

I got out of the car and walked toward the Kmart, but Hank didn't follow me. He couldn't leave, I figured, since I had the keys to the car and he knew I'd get lost in the city without him to navigate.

He was still there when I returned, sulking in the passenger seat. I laid my purchase out on the hood of the car, and I finally saw that he was paying attention.

"Don't do it, you crazy bastard," he cried out, stepping out from the vehicle. "Do you really wanna kill yourself?"

"It's a whole lot better than sitting in this damned car all night listening to you cry." I opened up the first package and readied myself for the first bite.

"That's poison!" he screamed, but I bit into it anyway. And though he was clearly scared, he could not stop me.

By the time he wrestled the last of it away from me, I had already devoured a brick and a half of sharp cheddar. We both knew what to expect next.

"Spit it up," my doctor yelled at me as I tried to get away from him by climbing up onto the hood of the Minnow. "Make yourself vomit. You gotta get that outta your system before it's too late. It's like when my dog got into my Halloween candy."

But, obviously, it was already too late.

"Do you see what you did?" I screamed at him. "Do you see what you *made* me do?"

Grasping me by the belt loops of my shorts, Hank tugged me back down to the pavement and snatched the cell phone from my pocket before I had a chance to swat him away.

"What's the phone number?" he demanded as he ran around to behind the car to evade me. "You've really done it this time. I'm looking in your phone for the number."

"Don't call my wife," I pleaded while chasing after him. "She'll never let me come back here by myself."

"I'm not calling her," he insisted as he climbed the back bumper to stand on the roof of our rental car while he pushed the buttons on the phone.

"Just take me to the emergency room to get my stomach pumped," I tried to compromise. "I promise I'll be good."

"Hello?" My doctor was speaking into the phone now. "Hi, this is Hank Matthews — Doctor Matthews. I'm friends with your son. He got into some cheddar again and I don't know what to do. Yeah, and I told him not to. Uh, I don't know, probably six pounds. Really? That should work? Okay, thank you."

That sonofabitch never should've gotten my mother involved, but at least he wasn't thinking about that old man anymore when his own best friend could be dying there right in front of him.

"Sprite," he said. "You need Sprite — some lemon-lime soda — and lots of it. Wait here; I'm going back into Kmart."

After he left, I tried to scavenge the rest of the uneaten cheddar, but it had been too badly tainted by a dirty sandal print and little bits of glass, sand and pebbles from the parking lot surface.

"Here, drink this," my doctor instructed upon his return, pushing a two-liter up against my face. "And you probably shouldn't drink any more of that eggnog."

"Are you all better now?" my doctor asked after I returned from the bathroom in the back of the bar and found a seat on the stool next to him. "Here, I ordered you a beer." He was drinking something big and red, probably sweet and fruit-flavored, and he appeared to have been crying.

This wasn't our first bar of the night — not even our first dive bar. But sweet fuckin' Christ, at least this place was tolerable.

We had to leave the respectable atmosphere of Jimmy Buffett's Margaritaville because Hank thought he heard the intro to a Wallflowers tune and it sent him into a frenzy. He tried to shove some douchebag wearing a sideways cap and lip ring over the upstairs railing. He was already good and drunk from several high-priced specialty margaritas, so all he needed now was something to maintain his intoxication. The last thing anybody wanted was Hank to lose his buzz and come crashing back down again.

"Come on," he ordered me after we left the Strip in the Minnow. "We need to find us some lowdown shithole, maybe over near the airport. I can't hear this trendy crap, not tonight. I need some Ted fuckin' Nugent."

That was alright by me, I told him. Quite frankly, I was growing tired of all the neon lights and drunk college kids. A dive bar might be good for us, and we found one on the outskirts of town. It was some place called the Wok & Woll, where they served Mongolian barbecue during the daylight hours and had drink specials and karaoke going once the sun went down. And it was there that my doctor had made a fool of himself.

The Wok & Woll was a place full of all sorts of scumbags and sleazeballs, people tired of the neon lights and drunk college kids on the Strip, people who just wanted to sink down in a corner booth and not worry about fitting in. It was a place where you could hear Asians pretend they were John Lennon on the karaoke machine, or watch some heavily inebriated man calling himself Chainsaw steal the microphone and for an hour straight make pretend that he's Jon Bon Jovi. It was a place that welcomed both homelessness and entrepreneurship, where, even past midnight, school children can mingle with the hobos and try to sell them all sorts of wondrous goods, from paper roses to candy necklaces.

"Howdy," said an elderly salesman as he approached our table with a suitcase full of miniature statues and an accent surely from Kansas or Missouri. "I carved all of these with my Skilsaw from a variety of hard woods. Tell me what you like. I have dogs and horses and monkeys."

"No, thank you," I waved him away, and without skipping a beat he moved on to the next table.

"Howdy," he said to his next potential customers. "I carved all of these with my Skilsaw from a variety of hard woods. Tell me what you like. I have dogs and horses and monkeys."

The place was perfect, I thought. Nobody would fuck with us there, and it would give Hank some time to wind down. But he needed more distraction, if only for a little while.

"There's a girl over there, and I think she's lost," I told him. "I think you should go over there and talk to her. She's actually pretty cute."

"Why don't *you* go over there and talk to her?"

"Because I'm still married, you asshole, and the cheese brick in my bowels has me partially paralyzed. Here," I said, slipping my wedding ring off my finger and handing it to him. "Girls love married guys. Go talk to her, buy her a drink, work your magic."

"She looks too high-maintenance. I don't want to get involved."

"Look," I explained to him, "you don't need a girlfriend. Just a quick fling." I ordered him a Jack & Coke to ensure he was still feeling right, and I badgered him into gulping it down fast.

"Alright, then," he finally agreed. "What happens in Vegas stays in Vegas. Except for the clap."

"That's the spirit," I encouraged, slapping him on the back. "Go tell her she's pretty, say you're in a band, and call me when you're done."

He half-stumbled over to her table and made himself at home. Clearly, a girl lost in a place like this is just looking for a one-night stand. Why else would she be here?

"What's your name, little girl?" he asked her. "What's your name?"

"Dawn," she smiled.

"You know, I was just thinking how I wanted to go to bed tonight and wake up at the crack of Dawn."

"Huh?"

"Never mind. I have to tell you," my doctor began again, "that you're the hottest girl I've ever seen." It was a good start, I thought, though not his best work.

"Even hotter than your wife?" she asked, pointing to the ring on his finger.

"Yeah," he smiled. "Even hotter than her. How about I buy you a drink, and then we'll go back to your place, or my place, and we practice making an imaginary baby."

That was one of my old pickup lines. It never worked for me, and it was only as I watched it from the outsider's perspective that I could understand why.

"Listen, fucker," she leaned in across the small table, tapping her pointer finger on the wedding ring he wore. "You're a cheating pig, and I just got out of a relationship with cheating pig like you, and I wouldn't let you fuck me with someone else's dick!"

"Well," Hank said, sitting back in his chair to better assess the situation, "I don't quite know what *that* means, but I'm not cheating. I'm not really even married. I'm just using this ring to pick up loose women. So, now that *that's* cleared up, let's get outta here. What kind of car do you drive?"

"You're a pervert," she told him, sliding her chair back and picking up her purse to leave.

"Shootin' you straight, little girl," Hank continued, unfazed. "Won't you do the same?"

"Look," she began to callously explain, "I saw you sitting over there, liked what I saw, and I was actually going to go over there and talk to you. I thought maybe you could ditch your retarded-looking friend, buy me a drink, and then you and I could hook up for the night. No strings attached, and no bullshit. Hell, I wouldn't have cared if you never even told me your name. But then you had to go and fuck it all up. What the hell is *wrong* with you?"

"What's *wrong* with me? No, I was just playing. I'm not even married. That sonofabitch put me up to it. I'm his doctor."

"No, you're an asshole. I'm going to the lady's room, and you'd better be gone before I come back, or I'm gonna tell the bartender I caught you trying to slip a roofie into my drink. You'll be dead before the cops get here."

Hank returned to our table, grabbed my arm and pulled me out of my chair.

"You should've told her you were in a band," I lectured him as we hurried out the door and hopped into the Minnow.

It was a rough start, I agreed, but even easy women aren't always as easy as they should be sometimes. That's just how life is.

"It wasn't your fault; you were drunk," I consoled Hank from atop the barstool at the second dive bar of the evening.

Hank starts off as a fun drunk — loud and obnoxious, just like regular people. But then, after he reaches the breaking point — the last stop before blackout — and something negative sets him off, he becomes angry, dangerous. He could kill someone.

Most people would make the mistake of cutting the drunk off, pumping him full of black coffee and then forcing him to sleep it off. This is definitely wrong as it simply promotes violence. The safest course of action is to encourage consumption, as much of it as possible in as little time as possible, to induce the inevitable blackout. As the responsible friend, however, you must remain absolutely sober during this process, or else what's the point? Nobody would be steering the ship. And I was nothing if not responsible.

"Did you put her up to it?" he accused me. "Did you *tell* her to hurt me like that?"

"No, I put *you* up to it," I reminded him. "And now she's off fucking somebody else, probably the bartender. Besides, you're drunk; it never would've worked out with her. Have another drink."

"That bartender stole my baby," my doctor continued to moan, and then he stood up, spilled his red fruity drink across the bar and stumbled for the door. "Come on. We're going back to Fremont Street to find that old lady. I'm getting married tonight."

Somewhere along the Strip, my doctor felt uncomfortable and climbed over the headrest to spread out in the back seat of the Minnow. As soon as his back hit the cheap fabric, he was fast asleep.

It's been my experience that you should never wake a drunk. There's no telling what sort of monstrosity he might morph into when robbed of his nap. With Hank, however, I knew he'd be a belligerent asshole, and so I let him sleep.

I parked again inside the structure beside the El Cortez. My doctor was snoring loudly behind me, and I knew a multi-level parking lot on the north side of town was not a safe place to sit and wait out Hank's eventual sobriety, so I left. I rolled up all the windows, pocketed the key and made my way out to the street.

By the time I crossed Las Vegas Boulevard, the canopy above Fremont was glowing and pulsating to a rock and roll tune and I ducked quickly into an A&W shop for a Coney Cheese Dog and a root beer. Then I gawked at some women for a while until they were clearly uncomfortable, and then I went back to the car.

Hank was still asleep when I got there, and I was still bored. *I should go back to the hotel room,* I reasoned, *where my accomplice could get proper rest in an actual bed and I could finally start working on my story.* My doctor was still not awake when I pulled the Minnow into the hotel parking lot, so I slammed the car door several times until he finally opened his eyes.

"Oh, good," I said. "You're awake. Let's get you back in the room before you puke on the upholstery."

But when we got to the room, our door was already open and our carpets were soggy, and each of the rooms around ours was in a similar state. A maintenance man came from a neighboring door and instructed us to pack up all of our personal belongings and see the hotel manager in the office. Hopefully she could get us another room.

"What a bummer," Hank signed. "I could really use a nap."

We shoved our clothes and shaving kits into our suitcases, and I was actually surprised to find my laptop and our two unopened cases of Budweiser still present. It was obvious our room door had been open for quite some time, and there was evidence of people having been in there while we were gone.

"Leave that Wallflowers CD here," Hank growled at me, but I packed it anyway. "Now what are we gonna do? It's too bad you decided to procrastinate writing your story."

"You fool," I countered. "I haven't yet begun to procrastinate."

The woman back at the hotel office was certainly no help to us.

"The place is flooded," she told us, as if we hadn't figured that much out on our own. "Water main broke someplace. Maybe it was a sewage pipe; I don't know. Looks like it Johnny Depped the whole second floor and some of the first."

"But you have extra rooms, right?" I inquired. "You're gonna move us to another room that's not flooded?"

"Sorry," she said. "No can do. We started moving people around a few hours ago. First come, first serve. But now we're out of rooms and we've been turning folks away."

"Bullshit!" My doctor was obviously not happy. I, on the other hand, had caught my second wind and wasn't as concerned with the situation as he was.

"Also," the woman continued, "you should really stay out of the pool. This issue with the plumbing, well, it all leads out into the pool. So you really don't want to be swimming out there for a few weeks at least."

"A few weeks? We're leaving here in a few days. Where are we going to sleep?" Hank was getting hostile, which he rarely ever is while sober and well rested.

"Hey," the hotel lady glared at us. "You guys didn't piss in your sink, did you?"

"Not me," Hank insisted.

"Regardless of where we pissed, where are we going to sleep tonight?" I was more concerned for Hank's sake, but I knew that having a hotel room to come back to was generally seen as a bit of a necessity. "We had reservations. We paid for this room!"

"Do you know who the fuck you're dealin' with?" Hank's temper was showing, so I sent him to the car with our stuff while I sorted out the mess with the desk lady.

"Well, obviously we're only going to charge you for the nights you've stayed here," she reasoned with me. "And, under the circumstances, I'm authorized to take fifteen percent off the tab. But I can see that you're not going to be satisfied with that, so I can also offer you a parting gift to alleviate any hard feelings so that you may come back and stay with us on your next visit to Las Vegas. Once we clean the pool out, obviously."

"Oh, obviously. What sort of parting gift?"

"How about two tickets to a Vegas show? We've got a top-notch entertainer in town, one night only. Why don't you and your doctor friend relax and enjoy the show on us?"

"Well, that doesn't sound too bad. Who's playing, Debbie Reynolds? Will we have to promise to stand quietly in the back and not smoke?"

Hank had already loaded our bags into the back seat of the car and was trying to relax in the front passenger seat when I returned with our prize.

"Eddie Money!" he exclaimed when I handed him the tickets. "Where at?"

"He's playing over at the college, some place called the Thomas & Mack Center. Sounds like a hot ticket. And the lady said that she was pretty sure we could get backstage to meet him."

"And it's only about twelve hours from now!" Hank exclaimed. "Let's go clean up in the bathrooms at the Encore, get a bite to eat and get over to the concert early to meet Eddie Money!"

It sounded like a fine idea to me, but the hotel lady rushed the car. I started it up and jammed it into gear.

"Gentleman, wait!" the hotel lady yelled as she rapidly approached in wobbly high-heel shoes. "Your credit card didn't go through, Mr. Zulu. I can give you the discount, but I'll need another form of payment."

"You fuckin' scoundrel," Hank yelled at me. "You were gonna make me pay halves on your fake credit card? You can't pull shit like that in Vegas. They'll hunt us down like dogs!"

"Not today, they won't." I jumped on the accelerator and gunned the little Nissan out of the parking lot and back toward the Strip. "Fuck 'em."

The parking lot at the college was surprisingly empty for an Eddie Money concert, especially considering we were slightly late. If there had been an opening act, we had surely missed it.

"No worries," Hank declared. "We'll just use our special tickets to go backstage and watch the show from the side of the stage."

"Good idea," I said. "That's better than front row."

But the man at the door there said the tickets were useless for anything other than regular general admission. Apparently, we'd been duped.

"Are you shitting me?" Hank screamed. "I drove all the way from New Orleans for this show. I was promised backstage access, and now you're telling me I have to sit out there with those lowlifes who probably didn't even pay for their tickets? Right here in my hand are two tickets to paradise. See?"

"Look," said the huge security guy, "it's not up to me. I work here and even I don't get to meet Eddie Money. You think I don't know how you feel? I have to stand here all night, I can barely hear the music and I sure as hell can't see the stage. And do I even get to shake Eddie Money's hand? No way. If I'm lucky, I can maybe score a t-shirt or a fuckin' beer koozie, or maybe a CD if nobody's looking."

"That's fuckin' rough," I sympathized. "But do you think you could just look the other way while we slip on through to the back?"

"Sorry, buddy. If I did that, I'd lose my job, and I need this job. I have kids."

"I hear you," I finally gave up. We went in through the proper doors and stood there in the back, watching as Eddie Money belted out a few classic tunes while the audience sat glued to their seats or stood motionless with dull stares.

"What the hell is this, a retirement home?" Hank blurted out. "This place is fuckin' dead. Do they not *know* who Eddie Money is?"

"Let's go get some beer," I said. "Then we'll watch the rest of the show. I just can't do this without at least a buzz."

We walked back out to the car, where we had waiting for us two cold and unopened cases of beer that needed to be consumed before it went bad. We decided to bring both cases inside to avoid having to make return trips.

"Hey, boys, you can't bring that in here." It was the security guard again. "No outside beer can be brought inside. Why don't you two nice, young fellas go get shitface-drunk in the parking lot and then come back inside and enjoy the rest of the show?"

"That's quite a walk, Carl," I replied, reading his name off his little badge. "And it's a lot of beer to pound in just a few minutes. You want some?"

"I wish I could, guys, but all I can drink is water and Coke, or else they'll fire me."

"Go grab a few koozies from the merchandise girls," I told him. "Nobody will know you're drinking beer."

"That's actually a good idea," he said. "Besides, this is just a part-time job. I don't care if they fire me, really."

He moved an orange road cone to where he was standing and disappeared behind a door, returning a few minutes later with a small plastic bag full of stolen goods.

"Here," he said, handing us each a koozie. We slid a beer into each of them and stashed the rest of the beer under a table near the front entrance that provided cover with a paper tablecloth. "You guys seem like good people. Nobody ever talks to the security guard. They all think I'm an asshole just for doing my job. I brought you guys some gifts from the back. They aren't autographed, but they're free."

Hank and I each received an Eddie Money tour t-shirt, which probably sold for more than twenty dollars apiece, and Carl gave us an Eddie Money greatest hits compilation CD to share. We immediately stripped out of the shirts we were wearing and tossed them at a trashcan, then slid into our new shirts, which were tight-fitting mediums.

"Sorry, boys," Carl apologized. "I didn't have time to check the sizes."

"No, these will work," I said. "You're a true friend, Carl. Enjoy those beers."

We slipped back into the concert and watched some of the show, but Hank was still annoyed by the overabundance of elderly audience members who apparently would have preferred to hear something quieter.

"Come on," he motioned toward the door. "We have a CD. We don't need these people."

And so we drove up and down the Strip for what must have been several hours, blasting Eddie Money from the speakers at full volume and smiling at the girls whose attention was drawn to our stylish cruising and the loud "woo" sounds we inexplicably yelled to them on the sidewalk.

"People just don't appreciate good music anymore," my doctor made his professional diagnosis from the parking lot of the Del Taco, where we posed against the hood of the Minnow to show off our shirts to people going in and out of the fast food joint. "They'd be jealous if it was Hannah Montana or the fuckin' Jonas Brothers."

"Those bastards forced their American Dream upon us, and it's sick," I concurred. "Come on. Let's go get a quesadilla."

"It's finally here," Hank said after digging through yesterday's newspaper over a Grand Slam breakfast at Denny's. "Ernesto Sandoval's obituary. The funeral's tomorrow afternoon."

"I thought you were off that," I said, still not interested in the dead guy but put off by the fact that my doctor was bringing it up yet again. "That waitress didn't bring me any Tabasco for my orange juice."

That old man was the last thing I wanted to deal with that early in the morning, especially with my hangover. The night before, we'd located a place on the strip that sold gigantic plastic bottles shaped like full-sized guitars and full of a thousand ounces of cheap beer. Refills were cost-effective, and we'd taken advantage of the fact.

"No, I'm not worried about it anymore," Hank assured me, "but it'd be nice to know if he's the same guy from the truck."

"Well, let's just assume it's the same guy, or that it's *not* the same guy, and then let's just forget about it. He was old. People die all the time. It was his time to go whether we were there or not."

"Keep your voice down," Hank whispered. "Somebody's gonna hear you and call the cops on us."

"Look," I said, lowering my voice a bit, "we didn't have anything to do with any of it. I'm not concerned, and I don't know why you are. Now, do you see our waitress?"

"I think we should go," Hank said, folding up the newspaper and setting it down on the seat beside him in the booth.

"Not until I finish my pancakes and get some Tabasco for my orange juice."

"No, I mean to the funeral. Why shouldn't we go?"

"You're asking me why we shouldn't go to the funeral of some complete stranger? Seriously? Do you not realize that we've been in Vegas for — *how many days have we been here?* — and we've spent surprisingly little time on the actual Las Vegas Strip? Doesn't that bother you at all?"

"I've seen the Strip plenty of times, and I'll see it again plenty of times," he said. "Hell, we still have plenty of time to see it before we leave here. We have no hotel room anymore and your fake credit card is no longer technically valid, so we can't afford another hotel room. We can go to the funeral and then spend the rest of the time on the Strip, like regular tourists."

"That's not a good idea."

"Then I'll just take the car for a while. I'll drop you off at Caesars Palace and call you once the funeral's done."

"Caesars Palace? You know that place scares me." I could see no other way out of this mess. If Hank is locked into an idea — any idea at all — it's nearly impossible to change his mind. This makes him the perfect victim of a pyramid scheme, but sometimes the worst companion for my fickle plans. "Fine, I'll go with you. But only if you promise me you'll drop it afterward, regardless of who's in the casket."

"It's a deal," he assured me. "We'll just sit in the back quietly and wait until the end. Then, once everyone walks past the coffin to pay their respects, we'll take a look to see if it's him. End of story."

"Fine. But what do you want to do until then? You wanna see if the Carrousel Bar is open?"

"No," he smiled. "Not only are we banned from that place still, but I have a special gift for you. Real Vegas entertainment."

"Cirque du Soleil?"

"Better," he said. "A magic show. It's not Penn & Teller, but it's top-notch. That's what the newspaper said, at least."

"I don't know," I told him. "Why should we spend our hard-earned money to watch some asshole make a tiger disappear?"

"Because it's free."

I couldn't argue with that. I was raised to be frugal, and I rarely ever pass up anything free. Hell, most of my household furniture was found on the side of the road and refinished in my shed with power tools and a quality dust cloth. Besides, beggars can't be choosers, and I was in desperate need of something to validate my paying money for a plane ticket to the wildest place on earth, even though a work assignment had been my initial excuse.

Oh, shit! My assignment!

"You can write about the magic show," my doctor reminded me. "It's good, clean fun for the entire family. It's something for both the tourist and the local resident. It's perfect."

And he was absolutely right, of course.

The Magnificent Aaron had a small stage tucked quietly between a couple of casinos off the Strip. From our view of the landscape, however, I couldn't quite remember where we turned in from and what establishments encased us on either side. *Did the gigantic wall belong to the Flamingo? Or was it the Tropicana? Maybe the Venetian?* They're all so different, but they're all so identical now.

Behind us were all manners of booths and carts, each selling some sort of carnival treat or offering caricatures drawn for a nominal fee.

What passed for a miniature amphitheater was full of folks of all ages in Wal-Mart rags, eager for a show but not willing to shell out the required fare to attend a performance by someone anybody has actually ever heard of before. This was budget-friendly Vegas.

"Fuck this," Hank said. "There's no seats left. I can't see a damned thing from this far back."

"Let's go backstage," I suggested. The Magnificent Aaron surely can't afford the level of security Eddie Money had.

But I was incorrect.

"Are you friends with Aaron?" the security guard asked as we casually tried to get past. He wasn't as big as Carl, but he looked to possess the capacity for more violence, even in his skin-tight yellow tee emblazoned with a unicorn under a fabulous rainbow.

"A friend of Aaron? Well, no," I explained. "But I think Hank here might be a friend of Dorothy."

"Who's Dorothy?" he asked. "I don't know no Dorothy."

"Well, never mind then. I'm actually here from the press. I'm writing a story on the Magnificent Aaron for the website and I need to speak to him."

"This is important, goddamn it!" Hank chimed in, slamming his fist against a flimsy sign announcing the upcoming magic show.

"Well, there's no time for that right now," the security guard told us. "Aaron's going on in a few minutes. Come back after the show and I'll let him know you're here."

"Sure thing," Hank said. "Maybe he'll let us know where he hides his tiger."

"Yeah," I encouraged my friend. "Maybe he'll let you pet it."

We once again found a place in the back, just outside the spectator area, and waited for the show.

It started off simple enough — an audience member plucked from the crowd picked a card from Aaron's deck and held it behind his back out of the magician's view. The Magnificent Aaron, sporting a beautiful top hat and a yellow shirt identical to that of his security guard, focused hard on the remaining cards, then wrote something on a large price of poster board with a Sharpie without showing it to the spectators or the woman with the pulled card.

"Yes or no, is your card the seven of diamonds?" Aaron asked loudly to the woman.

"No," she replied, to which the Magnificent Aaron turned around the poster board to reveal a large *NO* written in black marker.

The audience started to shuffle out in droves, so Hank and I each claimed a vacated seat.

"Alright then," Aaron continued, excusing the woman back to her seat in the audience. "I see that you folks aren't interested in mere léger de main. Who wants to see me pull a rabbit out of my hat?"

Nobody, of course, wanted to see him pull a fuckin' rabbit out of his hat, but that did not deter the Magnificent Aaron. So he carefully removed his beautiful top hat, held it upside-down in one palm and waved a small wand around the brim with his other hand, repeating some magic words I was sure he had ripped off from that blue talking head genie on *Pee-wee's Playhouse.*

The rabbit refused to show himself, so Aaron once again said the magic words and waved his magic wand. The rabbit, again, remained absent.

"Sonofabitch," Aaron mumbled as he tipped over his hat, from which a furry white lump dropped lifelessly onto the stage at Aaron's feet.

Members of the audience gasped and quickly filed out from the seating area with their children in hand, but the Magnificent Aaron was unbothered. He kicked the dead bunny hard to his left, where a stagehand scooped it up and carried it out of sight. Aaron motioned for an assistant to wheel out a large rectangular box and a huge chrome blade.

"This is better than David Copperfield," Hank exclaimed, climbing over the now empty seats to get a spot closer to the stage. I followed him, of course. I've always been a fan of magic shows, even though I put as much faith in their authenticity as I do professional wrestlers and TV chefs.

Opening the lid of the giant box, the magician motioned for his lovely assistant to lie down inside, which she did with a smile and sans any hesitation. The Magnificent Aaron closed the lid over her, then spun the entire contraption around three times before returning it to its original position.

"You ready, Katherine?" he asked his scantily clad sidekick, who returned a confident smile.

Aaron proceeded to position the large blade in the center of the box top, aiming it directly down onto the brave woman, then pushed his weight onto the thin metal device.

A blood-curdling scream echoed off the walls of the casino buildings around the tiny makeshift amphitheater as bright red liquid gushed from the sides and bottom of the box, signaling the remaining audience members to make a run for the exits. Stagehands quickly brought out a large white bed sheet and tried in vain to cover the bloody mess as only my doctor and I were left remaining in the seating area, standing on our chairs and clapping wildly.

"Get the hell outta here!" Aaron yelled at us while uniformed police officers rushed the stage and tackled the magician to the ground.

"Thank you for bringing me here," I smiled at Hank, admittedly the first genuine display of both gratitude and pleasure I had offered since arriving in Vegas. "Now let's get the fuck out of here before the cops make us explain shit."

I had to look up the directions to the church on my cell phone. We were dressed inappropriately for a funeral, obviously, but there was nothing that could be done about that. Paying my final respects to a guy I never even knew was clearly not on my agenda while I was packing my bags back in New Jersey. To be honest, in my excitement over the trip, I hadn't even packed clothes deemed appropriate for my job interview. But this was Vegas, after all, and so there was no sense of any amount of normalcy. Maybe my blue jean shorts, flip-flops and button-down Hawaiian shirt that barely covered a grease-stained wife-beater was just fine for both a meeting with a potential future employer *and* a funeral for a well-respected man of the city.

I drove the Minnow deep into the west side, past Bonanza Road and the ashes of the Moulin Rouge.

My doctor, meanwhile, was nervously brushing his teeth and spitting out the window of the car.

"Be careful with that," I warned him. "This isn't the Strip. This place is someone's home. And if they catch you spitting like that, we're liable to get shot."

"Park next to the building, by that side door," Hank instructed me as we came to the church. "I wanna be able to leave as soon as possible."

The parking lot was nearly empty as we were about an hour early. Hank was worried about getting there on time and I'm terrible with directions, even with my cell phone's GPS telling me exactly where to turn next.

"The coffin's probably already up front," I said. "If we get in there early, maybe we could just take a quick look and be on our way before anybody else gets here."

"That's actually a reasonable idea."

Having already positioned our getaway car near the side entrance, we decided it would be a safer route than the larger main doors facing the street since we wanted to avoid meeting any friends or family members of the deceased who might ask us questions regarding how we had come to know the dead man. But upon entering, our cover was blown when we were met by a white-haired priest who immediately handed us each a ten-dollar bill and ushered us into a back room. We took the money without question, because, well, it was money.

"I thought they couldn't find someone on such short notice," the old priest said as he closed the door behind us in the tiny room. "I don't think I know you. Is this your first time?"

"First time for what?" I asked nervously. "What

exactly are we doing here?"

"Damn it," the priest moaned. "I told them to send me someone who'd done this before."

"Maybe we should just leave," Hank offered politely, surely as confused as I was even though he had been in church many more times than I had growing up.

"No, you two will do just fine," the priest said. "Although, I have to admit, usually the boys are a bit younger."

"Alright then," I said, turning toward the door. "We'll just go outside and find you a couple of younger boys, some who look like they would keep their mouths shut. You're right; we're too old for you."

"Nonsense," he insisted. "I'm sure I could fit you in just fine."

"Oh, God," I said, fumbling with the doorknob but unable to get it to turn. "Oh, God. Take Hank, please, but let me go."

"Here, try these ones on," the priest ordered us, handing over a couple of white robes. "They should still be long enough to cover up those ridiculous sandals."

We took the robes and Hank slid into his. Still fearful of what might come next, I put mine on over my clothes and waited nervously.

"Alright," the old man continued, "I have to go make some last-minute preparations. You two get the thurible ready. The bell's on the table." Then he left us to wonder what the fuck was going on.

"I think we're altar boys," Hank determined. "What do we do now?"

"You're asking me? What the hell is an altar boy

supposed to do at a funeral? I say we just get the fuck out of here."

"No, we can't do that," Hank insisted. "This is actually perfect for us. We'll be right up front with the priest and the casket. All we do is stand there and hold the bell and the incense ball. It's easy. Besides, he already paid us."

"Why not?" I reasoned. We were already there, and we were wearing those spiffy robes. "Hey, we finally made it backstage someplace."

"How many of these incense things do we put inside?" Hank asked.

The incense ball was a little bigger than a grapefruit, had a base about the bottom and was attached to a section of decorative chain. On the table next to it and a bell was a box of those scented triangles burned at the homes of hip grandmothers and stoners.

"Just fill it up, I guess," I told Hank. "Stuff as many in there as you can fit."

It seemed like forever before the priest returned to the room to tell us that it was time to begin the service. He told us to stand in the wings during the beginning and to come on out when he nodded at us.

That was simple enough, I thought, but there were many small details we were not privy to, and neither Hank nor I ever thought to ask for a bit of clarification. So, once the priest was finished rambling on about Jesus and life and all manner of things like that, we received what we understood to be the nod and shuffled out onto the coffin staging area at the head of the church.

"Where do we stand?" I asked Hank under my breath.

"I don't know," he replied.

It was apparent by the priest's confused look that we were indeed misplaced, though he obviously felt it wasn't important enough to halt the service to correct us. Or maybe he was actually put off by the amount of smoke bellowing out from the incense ball Hank was dangling from the chain. I had lit it just before we stepped out from backstage, and it was immediately obvious that far fewer triangles should have been utilized.

I tried to distance myself from Hank and from the angry priest's death stare, but it was of no use. Though I backed away from the portable chimney in Hank's possession, the preacher man's eyes followed.

"Ring the bell," Hank mumbled to me. "I think he wants you to ring the bell."

And so I shook the bell once — *ku-ding* — and the priest offered a half-assed smile and nod before returning to his death speech. Several minutes later, he was staring at me again. *Ku-ding.* Then once more down the line — *ku-ding* — and I began to consider abandoning my job interview altogether and go into business for myself as a traveling Catholic funeral bell-ringer boy. Charging ten dollars per show would keep my budget tight, but I could find a way to make it work.

"Hey," Hank called quietly to me. "Ring the bell."

I looked up to see the priest glaring at me with a stare that could fry a man's brain. And so I rang the bell, and I rang it good. *Ku-ding!* But the holy man did not look satisfied, and so I rang it again. *Ku-ding!* And then I rang it again, and again, and then I shook the fuck outta that goddamn bell — *ku-ding, uh-ding, uh-ding, uh-ding, uh-ding* — and I didn't stop ringing until the priest walked over to me and snatched the bell from my grasp and angrily slammed it down onto the lid of the coffin beside us. The force of the hit shook the box hard enough to knock over a small flower arrangement that had been placed beautifully on top of the coffin, and the display scattered messily at the priest's shoes.

It was only then that I realized it was a closed-casket funeral and that it would take some work now to see the body. I glanced over to Hank to see if he had ever noticed the lid was closed, and I could see that he too was worried. It probably wasn't the closed lid that had him concerned so much as the thick black fumes that surrounded him and the ball he dangled from the chain.

"You little bastards," the holy man snapped at us under his breath, though not quite muffled enough for the funeral guests to disregard. "You're ruining everything!"

The incense had really become engulfed by then, and the mourners were finding the putrid stench harder to ignore. Some in the first few pews were fanning themselves with their bibles while a small number of them actually stood up and moved toward the back of the church for fresher air.

"That ain't right!" a middle-aged Hispanic man yelled after jumping to his feet in the first pew and pointing at Hank.

"Get them outta here!" yelled a woman from a few rows back.

"They're doing it on purpose," screamed another man who glared directly at me. "That one there is smiling!"

"Hey," Hank whispered to me. "Stop smiling."

"Please, folks," the priest tried to calm the mob. "We're just having some technical difficulties." Then he turned to us and shot, "You're in a world of shit now, boys. Not even God can save you from these folks."

My doctor was of no help. I could see in his eyes that he was void of any suggestions.

"Hike up your dress," I said to him. "Let's get the fuck outta here!"

We darted off to the left of the raised platform, but the priest grabbed onto Hank's sleeve and spun him around in the opposite direction. I latched onto his other sleeve and broke him free and the three of us made a full lap around the coffin and shot out down the wide center aisle toward the large main doors.

Just as we saw our freedom in sight, Hank was tackled from behind by the priest and I could feel him tug on the back of my altar boy robe as he went down. I quickly thought of leaving him there to fend for himself, but I knew he'd rat me out to the cops once they inevitably arrived to haul him away. I turned around to assist in his getaway, but was decked squarely in the left eye but what appeared to be a professional prize fighter in a black suit.

I was clearly disoriented, but I latched onto Hank's outreached hand and dragged him out the door and down the steps toward the street. Once Hank was back on his feet, we both started back toward the car in a sprint, but it wasn't until I was safe inside that I realized my doctor had fallen somewhere behind. I inserted the key into the ignition, revved up the Minnow and threw it into gear. I screeched in reverse from my parking space and whipped the front of the tiny car around in trademark James Rockford fashion, then slammed onto the accelerator and jumped onto the sidewalk in front of the church.

Hank was curled up in the fetal position near the curb and the lynch mob dispersed once they saw the red Nissan shooting straight for them. All who remained was Hank and the priest, who was now using the incense ball as one would a medieval flail, holding the chain and whipping the smoking weapon down hard repeatedly onto Hank's spine.

Blasting the horn, I landed the Minnow between them and the crowd, and the priest took to beating the hood of the car and windshield with his scented weapon. My doctor opened the rear door and crawled into the seat and onto the suitcases behind me, and I locked the doors as the crowd surrounded the vehicle, kicking and pounding at it while I tried in vain the drive away.

"That fucker maced me," Hank whined as he tended to a bloody nose.

The Minnow fared far worse than Hank, however, as dents were kicked into the thin sheet metal on all sides of the car. The passenger-side mirror was ripped the rest of the way off the vehicle and the left rear door window was cracked just above where Hank covered his head in his hands. Fists and feet and elbows pummeled against the Nissan and we were completely surrounded.

"Drive!" Hank screamed at me, but there was no way for me to go without running somebody over. Accidental desecration of a Catholic funeral was one thing, but vehicular homicide was much more than I cared to answer for.

Soon, the car was rocking as mourners on both

sides attempted to flip it over onto its roof. With only the left or right tires touching the ground at any given time, I knew it wouldn't be long before the sardine can was permanently immobilized. I pressed on the horn and jumped on the gas pedal. The lynch mob threw itself out of the way as the car took off on its left wheels, performing some sort of circus show routine until Hank bounced to the right side of the back seat and leveled the ride.

I entered onto the first road we came to and headed straight without looking back.

"Are they following us?" I asked my travel companion.

"I don't know. How can I tell?"

"Well, is there a classy black station wagon coming at us doing a hundred miles per hour?"

"No," he said. "Just keep driving before they call the cops."

We finally stopped the car when it ran out of gas out in the middle of nowhere. I didn't even know where we were anymore, and my sleazebag doctor was certainly of no help.

"I think we're north, but we may actually be south," he determined. "What do we do now?"

"I'll steer the car," I told him, "and you'll push. There has to be a gas station up the road a bit."

"Why don't you push the car?" he whined. "You got us into this mess."

"Because I have a swollen fuckin' eye, that's why."

And so while peering down the desolate stretch of crumbled blacktop with my one good eye and trying to ignore the John Bonham solo taking place between my brain and skull bone, I guided the car along until we came to the outskirts of what might have actually been a quaint little town at one time. As

111

we approached an old gas station, a few men hurried over and assisted Hank in pushing the car toward the pumps.

"How the hell did you run out of gas?" an older and particularly grizzled local inquired. "I just don't think I've ever seen someone actually *do* that in real life before. Where you going? You headed out to Creech? If so, you're a little off course."

After explaining that we had been attacked by a pack of drug-crazed street thugs, the people there gathered around the car to assess the damage.

"Nice car. She looks fast," grinned a nearly toothless young redheaded girl as she spat out a mouthful of tobacco juice. "What kinda engine you got in there?"

"Uh, well, it's got a 396 Holley dual cam barrel," I explained to her, "with a four on the floor and a fifth under the seat."

"Sound like hell on wheels," she smiled before spitting again. "How about you take me for a ride in that race car of yours?"

"Well, I'd like to, but I think I need to get something to drink first. I had to push this car all the way in from the Strip, and I'm awfully tired."

As Hank panted in exhaustion and dehydration from having actually done the hard work over the past few miles, some of the older men offered to tape up our car the best they could while we took a rest in the diner up the block. So, after we filled the tank, we parked the car in front of the service station and let them go at it.

As we entered through the old wooden doors, I felt like I was walking into the saloon in an old western movie. Everyone inside the place stopped what they were doing and stared at us until we took our seats at a rickety old table in the middle of the restaurant. Then they all went back to their coffee and conversations as if we were now invisible.

"I'll be back in a minute," Hank said, standing back up and looking around the place. "I just need to use the bathroom."

"The bathroom, you say?" called over an old gold miner. "It's in the back, over there, but be mindful of the John Wayne toilet paper. It's rough and gritty, and it don't take shit off nobody." And then the entire diner erupted in a fit of laughter for exactly twenty seconds before falling collectively silent once again.

Hank left me alone there for a while longer than I had hoped and a wiry young guy with a mop of dirty auburn hair and a sleeve he'd obviously been using as a snot rag came over and sat down in the vacant seat across the table from me.

"I know I just met you and all," he started, "but you look like a fella I could trust, right?"

I nodded, but only because trust seemed very important to these simple folks and I really didn't want to make enemies with another population of people.

"My mom, you see, she operates this daycare outta her living room," the guy continued. "Well, one day, and this was years ago so the statute of limitations is all runned out, but she had this retarded kid that she took care of. For the sake of the story, we'll just call him Crackers. And when I was a kid I'd sneak some cigarettes outta my mom's purse. I still do that sometimes, but only when I don't have no more of my own. But anyways, this one time I was playing with Crackers, bouncing him on my knee and such, and one of the cigarettes fell outta my pocket. Well, Crackers wanted it, and so I let him have it. He ate it and wanted another one, so I went and got the pack outta my mom's purse and I fed him every one of the cigarettes she had left in the pack. And then Crackers went to sleep, and he never woke up. My mom lost her daycare license from the county and she had to get another one in my brother's name. But when I go to sleep, sometimes I still see Crackers' face, drooling all over me as he bounces on my knee. I didn't know cigarettes were poison to retarded kids like chocolate is to dogs, and that's the honest truth."

I didn't say anything. What the fuck *could* I have said to that? As he finished his story, Hank returned from the bathroom and the guy stood up from the chair.

"Don't you tell him what I told you," the young guy told me as he moved aside so Hank could sit back down. "If you tell him, I'll fuckin' kill ya."

"I won't tell anyone," I reassured him, and he walked out the saloon doors and down the street.

The waitress said she knew just what we needed and brought us each a large glass of Coke and a sloppy joe sandwich. The food was questionable, but we ate it anyway. These people scared us and it was wise to not insult them.

"Lunch is on the house for a couple of nice fellas like yourselves," the waitress said while she cleared away our empty plates.

We thanked her, nodded to the rest of the patrons who were staring unapologetically at us, then casually but carefully strolled to the door and out onto the crumbled sidewalk.

"We've wandered into a fuckin' time capsule," my doctor assessed. "The car has gas. Let's get the fuck outta here."

The Minnow was taped up nicely. In place of the stolen passenger-side mirror, the townsfolk had affixed one borrowed from another vehicle, possibly from the junk yard behind the gas station. The shattered window was gaudy but structurally sound beneath multiple layers of gray duct tape, and the bumpers were stuck back where they should have been. It would never pass a safety inspection, but that was of no concern to us. It would surely stand out in traffic, especially if those zealots from the funeral home called the police on us.

The gas station parking lot was empty, and so was the garage. I told Hank to locate whoever had our key while I cleaned the windows. As I began to squeegee the windshield clean with the murky black water from the bucket next to the pumps, I saw a monster appear along the road near the patch of weeds and desert across the street from the service station.

It was gigantic, like a Great Dane or a small horse, but it had the face of a bald coyote and the armored backside of a triceratops. It looked mean, but its short legs told me that it probably couldn't jump very high. Armed with the squeegee, I went in for a closer look.

It snarled at me as I approached, then lunged at my feet, sniffing my flip-flops and wiping snot on my toes. I backed up quickly, but it followed, smiling through its greasy lips and obviously smelling my fear as I fell backward onto my ass. I jumped to my feet and whacked it once on the forehead with the

115

squeegee handle. The monster was stunned, but not for long, and it lunged at me again.

I knew I could not penetrate its armored back with a squeegee, so I went for the head, whacking it over and over again as hard as I could while it grunted and whined like a baby pig. This may have been the fat, angry father of La Chupacabra for all I knew, and there was no way I was going to stand by and let it eat the townsfolk who were so generous and hospitable to me.

Just as I delivered the deathblow, I looked over to see Hank retrieving the car key from the bearded man who had taped up the Minnow. As they shook hands, I threw the squeegee handle high above my head and gave a victorious "Woooo!"

"What your strange friend doing over there?" the bearded man asked Hank, but Hank could not answer.

I jogged over to the two of them and explained how I had just saved the down from a ferocious beast.

"A beast?" the puzzled man asked. "The only beast around here is Lester."

"What's Lester?" Hank questioned cautiously.

"Lester's our town mascot. A giant armadillo. Jake Abbot brought its great-granddaddy back from Texas when he was stationed out there during the Great War. What the hell did you *do* to ole Lester?"

The bearded man sprinted across the street to the battle scene, paused, then yelled out, "You killed Lester, you motherfucker!"

As the townsfolk shuffled out of the diner and the post office and the general store to make sense of the commotion, Hank and I ran to the car and started it up. By then, the bearded man was instructing the other citizens to stop us in our tracks, and the lynch mob hurried over to the Minnow. I threw it into gear and burned out of the gas station parking lot, flinging sand and gravel at the angry crowd before tearing off down the road into the direction from which we had pushed the car.

"Well, that's the last of my money," I said from a seat in front of a Caesars Palace slot machine. "I'm officially broke. How much money do you have left?"

"Including all the returns from my previous investments and what I have in savings, I have a grand total of four dollars." Hank searched through his pockets once more but could not add to that amount. "This is all we have left to live off of until we get back home."

"We'll go halves," I told him. "We'll drop it in the slots. It couldn't get much worse. We could always panhandle in front of some gas station someplace."

"I sure as hell don't wanna have to call my dad to have him wire me money," Hank said.

I put my two dollars in first, and promptly lost it. Hank, at the machine next to me, won big on his first pull — eight hundred dollars. The *ding-ding-ding* and the flashing lights of the machine made a few nearby slot gamblers look our way as the machine spit out a receipt. Sure, it wasn't the millions that everybody hopes for, but it wasn't small change to a couple of hungry bums like Hank and me.

"Shit, boy, how much did you put in there?" cried an excited old man in the next seat over.

"That was my first dollar," Hank told him, clutching onto the receipt so it couldn't be ripped from his hands before he could cash it in.

"Well, damn it all!" the man yelled to the ceiling. "I'd get up and jump up and down with ya, but my legs won't work proper. I've been sitting here for too long. Two days at this same machine, just waiting for it to pay out. Turns out I was sitting at the wrong machine."

"Maybe someone else won on your machine when you got up to use the bathroom," I tried to console the poor bastard. "It's not your fault. You can't just sit here twenty-four hours a day."

"Colostomy bag," he said, raising one pant leg to reveal a clear sack full of amber-colored piss strapped to his ankle. "It's an old trick. I do this for a living, but I've been in a rough patch lately. Boys, I can honestly say that I know what Old Mother Hubbard's dog felt like."

"Stay strong," I said, patting him gently on the shoulder. "Things will turn around for you."

"What the hell do you know?" he growled as he stood up on his wobbly legs. "If you don't mind, I'm gonna go home now and shoot myself in the mouth."

After cashing in his winnings, Hank kept to his word and went halves, supplying us each with a wallet full of twenties.

We now had enough money to legally pay for a hotel room. We weren't looking for a place to sleep, but rather a place to shower and brush our teeth. With this little bit of good luck finally coming our way, I found the motivation to write my story. I started typing while Hank showered and I was finished by the time he returned to the room with a full bag from Del Taco.

"All finished," I said proudly before slurping down my quesadillas. "Our luck has changed. Let's keep this momentum going."

"That's my feeling exactly," my doctor concurred. "Let's go shopping. We both need some new clothes. I wasn't expecting to get this dirty, and you have that job interview."

I took advantage of the hotel's free Internet access and emailed my article to my potential future employers. By the time I showered and got ready to go, they had emailed me back and asked me to come in for the interview later that same day.

"That's cutting it close," Hank said. "We're supposed to fly outta here tomorrow. It's a good thing you finished it on time. You really think they'll hire you?"

"Look who you're talking to. Who writes better than I do?"

Though we did strike it big recently, we decided to remain conservative with our shopping and headed to Wal-Mart. I got a nice pair of khaki shorts, a midnight blue polo shirt with a pocket on the breast and a clean pair of flip-flops. Hank, dissatisfied with anything without an alligator logo, bought the white trash equivalent.

"You'll need to look more professional than that," my doctor informed me. "They'll never hire you looking the way you do."

I found a cheap briefcase in the luggage department and a six-dollar pen to display protruding from my shirt pocket. I thought about going with socks and shoes instead of sandals, but Hank agreed that it would send the wrong message, as if I was trying too hard to conform. After my work ensemble was complete, we were on our way.

We dined at a nice Italian place, had a few beers, then killed some time in a pawn shop on the Strip beyond the Stratosphere. Hank purchased a lug nut that supposedly came from James Dean's Porsche and I paid seven dollars for a pair of handcuffs to attach the briefcase to my wrist. In the briefcase were all of my valuables, including my laptop, Wallflowers CD and my stack of remaining cash.

I looked the part of a professional journalist, and now all that there was left to do was secure that title with a successful job interview.

We navigated our way through a series of back roads and side streets until we finally came to the home office.

"I don't think this is the right place," Hank said. "I think your phone's GPS is broken."

"Maybe, but I double-checked the address, and it still says this is the right place."

It didn't look like the kind of building a magazine would be published from, online or not. It looked more like an abandoned hospital. Our suspicions were confirmed when we noticed some old white paint had peeled and fallen from the wall above a side entrance revealing an ancient sign stating "Ambulance Parking Only."

"Another fuckin' time capsule," Hank grumbled. "I bet this place is older than Vegas itself."

The building was small, so it was certainly possible that bigger digs were required decades ago that forced the hospital to move to a more modern facility to meet the city's growth, but if it wasn't for the bright sun still above our heads and the normal traffic zipping past on the street behind us, it would appear that we were heading into the setting of some Stephen King novel.

The creepiness didn't dissipate once we entered. The lights overhead flickered and hummed and we passed by what must have once been a nurse's station and small waiting room. Hank picked a magazine up from a bench and shook it off, which sent a thick cloud of dust into the air around us.

"This magazine's forty years old," he said before tossing it back down. "This can't be the right place."

The dead silence was broken by the sound of a rusty squeak from the other end of a long corridor just past the nurse's station. Slightly scared, we peered down the hallway and could make out the silhouette of a hunched over object slowly making its way toward us.

"Are we running away again?" my doctor asked. "I don't mind running away just one more time."

But before I could answer, the figured broke free from the darkness and I could barely make out a man in a wheelchair, still creeping up slowly. I wasn't able to see his face clearly, but he really wasn't making it easy for me.

"A zombie?" I asked Hank. "You're a doctor. How the hell do you kill a zombie? A silver bullet or a stake in the heart?"

When the wheelchair stopped, Hank and I started to back slowly toward the door. We were both smart enough to know that the movies always portrayed zombies incorrectly as slow and stumbling. In actuality, the undead gain strength and mobility and it's very difficult to outrun a zombie once it begins a sprint.

"You boys here for an interview?" the zombie spoke as it stood from the wheelchair and began to slowly walk our way. "The office is over this way."

"Are you gonna eat us?" Hank called out.

"What the hell are you talking about?" the creepy dude replied. "Is one of you Victor?"

It was only after we made it down the hallway and into the one fully lit room in the entire building that we could see the type of operation they had set up. There were five functioning computers on small desks and a large screen television attached to the wall in one corner. There were printers and a fax machine, four telephones and a mini refrigerator, all hastily crammed in wherever they could fit.

The zombie man we met in the hallway had found a seat in another wheelchair behind one of the desks and his business partner was lying down on an old gurney, taking sips from a tube that was fed from a beer bottle hanging upside-down from an IV rack.

"What the hell happened to your eye?" The guy in the chair asked, but he didn't wait for a response. "Is your name really Victor Zulu, or is that some stupid pen name?"

I reached for my wallet and produced an Arizona driver's license identifying me by that name and handed it to him.

"So it is," he said before handing it back to me. "For some reason, we just figured that a guy named Zulu would somehow be, uh, darker."

But there it was, right there in legal form, and with my picture on it. The license was about eight years old, but it was still good. It can sometimes take several decades for an Arizona driver's license to expire, and I'd be an old man before I ever had to argue about the validity of that particular moniker.

I had met a girl in a Yuma bar once who told me she worked for the motor vehicle division. So, of course, I dated her for a few weeks and then asked her to do me a solid favor. If caught, she would have been fired for sure, possibly even prosecuted, but I could be quite charming when I had to be. It was a talent that I could turn on and off like a light, though the switch seems to have been stuck in the off position for quite a while.

Anyway, I got my new identification, made up some sob story about being transferred to another state, and had to avoid her favorite bars for the rest of my tenure in Yuma.

But it was worth it. The credit card, the hotel room, the Minnow — none of it would have been possible without the help of that poor little pudgy girl with the low self-esteem and an overwhelming desire to please those she really cared about.

"Well, I'm Jeff, and that over there is Sam," the clean-cut thirty-something guy in the wheelchair told me. "We operate this whole organization. We're not online yet, but we hope to be by the end of the month. This place here is just temporary. It was cheap and vacant, and we needed the square footage. Once we really get going, secure some more sponsors, we'll move someplace more desirable, maybe someplace downtown."

"That's good to hear," I said. "I'm really looking forward to the opportunity to write with you guys. I did have one question, though."

"Go for it," Jeff grinned.

"Well, in the listing, you never really mentioned what you would be paying."

"Whoa," Jeff cut me off, standing from his wheelchair and picking up a printout of the article I had emailed to him earlier. "Nobody ever said you had the job just yet. We read over your story earlier, *after* we invited you in for the interview, and I do have to say that Sam and I were both a bit concerned."

"Concerned about what?" I inquired sheepishly.

"It sucks," Sam finally contributed to the conversation before replacing his beer tube at the corner of his mouth and closing his eyes again.

"No, I wouldn't go so far as to say that it sucks," Jeff continued. "Well, actually, it *does* suck. I mean, your write well, you know where a comma goes, you know what a semicolon does, and you seem to know a little bit about the inverted pyramid structure, but the content is just no good. It's no good at all."

"You told me to write about Las Vegas, and that's what I did."

"Yeah, but it's just no good." He slapped the papers down on his desk and took his seat. "Crazy men in Chinese food restaurants, slaying monsters, destroying funerals, jumping cars, Del Taco, scaring old men to death — there's liability issues here, to say the least. This isn't what we wanted at all. Don't get me wrong, it looks like you put a lot of time and effort into it, and I'm probably going to forward the email around to some of my friends for laughs, but it's just not right for a respectable and reputable local publication."

"Your story has too many holes in it. It's just like my socks," Sam said. "Tell them about my socks, Jeff."

"There's a lot of holes in his socks," Jeff explained. "You can see his feet right through them. It's unsightly, really. I keep telling him to buy new ones, or just go barefoot, for fuck's sake."

"But it's all real," I tried to counter before being cut off again.

"I'm not so sure it *is* real. Besides, even if it's real, that's not what our core demographic wants to read about. They wanna see Vegas as a safe place to live and a fun place to play. They don't wanna read about racism and violence. Don't you understand? Las Vegas is the epicenter of the American Dream."

And just like that, I did understand. The goddamn American Dream had finally smothered the last breath out of the one place I hoped was strong enough to withstand the pressure.

"Here," Jeff continued, "let me find you an example of what we're looking for here." He picked through the mess on his desk before turning to ask his intoxicated partner for some help. "Where is it, Sam? The one by that one guy — Bryant something-or-other."

Sam gulped the last of the beer through the tube and sat up to look for the papers, eventually finding them crammed underneath him on the gurney.

"Have a gander at that masterpiece," Sam mumbled as he handed me the wrinkled mess. Then he retrieved another beer from the fridge, replaced the empty and plopped back down on the gurney.

I looked at it, but I was really in no mood to read anything deemed superior to my own work, and Hank was offering no help with my case.

"Read it," Jeff insisted, though he proceeded to provide me with a brief summary. "That story is about life here in Las Vegas. This old fella — more than a hundred years old — he's been saving every ticket stub to every movie he's ever seen since the invention of movies. He saw all the quiet ones, and he even saw that talking one with the piano player. He even sat through movies he knew he'd hate because they have Jim Carrey in them, just so he could collect the ticket stubs. And he put them in scrapbooks to pass on to his children and grandchildren and he graded each movie on a scale of one through ten and wrote it next to the stub. This guy's one of the original movie critics of the entire world, and he's living right here in Clark County and nobody ever knew he existed until this Bryant fella decided to write about him. Now he's gonna be in the history books."

"Are there any movies there with Loretta Young?" Hank had finally decided to join in. "I'm related to her."

"Well, I don't know," Jeff answered. "But maybe with all the attention our publication will get him, this old man will decide to compile all his scrapbooks and publish them and you could read the book in its entirety to find out. Wouldn't that be something?"

"Gee, it sure would!" Now even Hank was on board.

"Fuck that!" I shouted. "You wanna turn Vegas into Mayberry. What the fuck do you guys know about journalism? You don't know shit. You're looking for an easy buck and you're willing to rape your readers just to please some bullshit sponsors. You're fuckin' lame and pathetic."

"I think someone's trying to pull a fast one here," Hank agreed.

"You're just pissed that you're a shitty writer and that nobody will ever read your work," Jeff argued back. "You're fuckin' fired, you dumbass. I never even considered hiring you, but you're still fired. Now get the fuck outta my office."

"Want me to kick their asses, Jeff?" Sam asked as he attempted to sit up from his gurney. "I'll give that motherfucker another black eye."

But before he could steady himself in an upright position, Hank grabbed the side of the gurney and flipped it upside-down, sending the drunken douchebag to the ground under the overturned bed.

"That's it!" Jeff yelled as he picked up a telephone receiver. "I'm calling the cops."

"The cops don't care about shit like this, Jeff!" I teased the spoiled rich kid. "This is Las fuckin' Vegas. You haven't killed it yet!"

Using the briefcase still chained to my wrist, I knocked everything from the top of Jeff's desk and on our way out of the building, I flung a wheelchair down the hallway. Laughing off our tantrum, we climbed back into the Minnow and I steered it back toward the neon lights to hopefully enjoy the rest of the stay, which was by then simply a vacation and no longer any sort of business trip.

We felt victorious after holding our own in the screaming match, but in truth I had been once again defeated.

"You don't need them, anyway," my doctor tried to console me from a table on the second floor of Jimmy Buffett's Margaritaville. "You don't wanna live in a place like Vegas. The novelty would wear off quickly. You come here once or twice a year, live it up, them go home and think about the next time. If you live here, you'll only see the bad parts and you'll have nothing else to look forward to."

"Smoke and mirrors," I agreed. "I guess the trick is to not stay here long enough to see the smoke clear."

And that's all it was.

Living in the residential areas around Vegas is probably a lot like living around Disney World.

There's the thrill in knowing that a massive playground is right in your backyard, but the circus act that is inevitably attached to such an environment can be annoying at times and even intrusive. There's no sense of normalcy, if that's what you desire at some point in the future.

There's plenty of history, but there's no trace of it outside of old photos and stories. Everything is torn down and built back up; long-term residents just accept it, and their idea of "regular" is skewed along the way. There's no coffee and donuts on your way to the office. You get a scotch on the rocks, a quick pull of the machines, then head into work.

"You wanna give me one of your stupid metaphors?" Hank asked. "They never make any sense to me, but you seem to understand them."

"What do you wanna hear, something about waves crashing and seeing the tide break?"

"No, I guess not. But we only have one more day left, so let's drink and make the most of it. This is still Las Vegas. We'll have a good time, the way it was intended when God established this good city a thousand years ago, and then you'll have something to write about once you get home."

"I don't think I'll do that any time soon," I said. "Whatever I write would be boring and nobody would believe it."

"Just the same, you should probably change my name. I wouldn't want my fame to get in the way of my medical practice."

I considered it, and then we placed our order with the waitress. I started with my usual Jack and Coke, but we were soon both downing specialty margaritas and various fruity beverages, along with oddly named shots and straight tequila.

"We can't waste any time here," I told my doctor. If they notice we're intoxicated, I think they're required by law now to cut us off and throw us to the curb."

"You're right," Hank said. "It's best to order a whole bunch at one time, then down them all quickly so that when it finally hits us, it'll hit us quick and hard."

After a friendly discussion-turned-argument about whether Diamond Dave or Sammy Hagar was the better Van Halen vocalist, the waitress brought us our check, even though we hadn't asked for it. I remember it was something like three hundred and twenty dollars, but I don't remember actually paying for it. I do remember, however, standing on the sidewalk somewhere on the strip, almost coming to blows with Hank and then accusing a passerby of being Gary Cherone. After the passerby shoved me hard to the ground and threw his beer at Hank, my memory faded even more.

I remember talking on a payphone someplace, which is weird because I had a perfectly good cell phone in my pocket. I don't remember who it was I had talked to, but I do remember they were angry. And that just made me angry.

I recall sprinting across the Strip in flip-flops, narrowly dodging honking automobiles, and I do know that I purchased more cigarettes at a convenience store and then one of those giant guitar-shaped beer containers from some little outside bar.

I remember dancing — though I never dance — and I may have been kicked in the stomach at some point by a small gang of disgruntled tourists.

The few moments that I am able to recall are seen from someone else's point of view, like some sort of out-of-body experience. Someone had to witness it, I guess, but it sure wasn't Hank. My scumbag doctor ditched me someplace when I wasn't looking, but I don't think I noticed or cared at the time.

There was music — Jimi Hendrix, Britney Spears, then Nick Drake?

What the fuck? Where was I? Was I dead?

I woke up on a bench along the Strip near the Mirage. That's something simply not tolerated in Las Vegas and I'm still not sure why I wasn't hauled away by the police for either vagrancy or public intoxication. I could've just as easily woken up on a police cot with some actual criminals, though judging from my broken memories of the night prior, I may have done some things to earn that title myself.

At first I thought that I might not have been there long, that maybe I had just recently plopped down for a quick rest and, in the process of doing so, woken from my blackout. But then, as I took off my sunglasses to wipe the beads of sweat from my face, I realized that I had been there for quite longer, possibly even hours, just frying in the morning sun like a thick strip of center-cut bacon. A quick glance at my arms and legs confirmed this, as all of my exposed skin was as bright red as my rental car.

Shit. Where's the car? And where the fuck is Hank? I could sure use a doctor right now, even a fake one.

But that bastard was nowhere around. I couldn't remember the last time I'd seen my friend, and I sure as hell couldn't account for my right forearm feeling like it was on fire beneath a taped-on bandage. I peeled off the pad to reveal a fresh new tattoo of what I could only assume was Asian writing.

I sat there on the bench, dazed and pondering my next course of action. As the typical-looking crowd of tourists scurried past, not giving me so much as a second glance, I spotted an Asian couple and decided to have them translate the tattoo for me.

"Hey," I said, stopping them in their tracks. "Are you Chinese?"

"No, we're Korean," the male Asian said.

"Close enough. Can you tell me what this says?"

"I think it's jin long," the female one spoke up. "I think I saw it on our way into town. Try the eggrolls."

"Motherfucker," I grunted as I turned away and found my place back on the bench. I was thirsty and glancing around for a place to hydrate with a cold beer when my cell phone began ringing in my pocket.

"Where the fuck are you?" Hank screamed at me as soon as I answered. I've been calling you for hours."

"The Mirage. Where are you?"

"I'm with the car at the MGM. I'm out of money. You have the car key. Get the fuck over here." And then he hung up.

When I got to the top level of the MGM Grand parking structure, Hank was sprawled out on the hood of the Minnow and I could tell that he was not happy with me, but all seemed forgotten once he saw my glowing flesh.

"Shit, man, what the hell happened to you?"

"I don't know," I said. "I was hoping you could fill me in."

"How the hell would I know? Last time I saw you was after you took a hit from that cigar."

"Cigar? What cigar?"

"From those three black kids. Don't you remember?"

What the hell was he jabbering on about? I'd chain-smoked cigarettes since we arrived in Vegas, but I never smoked any cigar. At least not that I could recollect.

"Sure, you remember all right," he continued. "We were outside, you puked on a valet sign, then those three black kids asked you for a light. You handed them your lighter, then they offered you a hit off their cigar. First I told you not to do it, thought maybe you'd pop on a drug test at work, but then I remembered that you don't have a real job. So you took a puff, punched me in the throat and took off. I never heard from you again."

"Well," I shrugged, "that would really explain some things, I guess."

"Yeah, and then you didn't answer your cell phone and I spent the whole night wandering around looking for you. I went into Bally's and got lost in there for hours. I somehow ended up in the hotel hallways, probably tripping off of a contact high from the cigar smoke. I was surrounded by all kinds of ghosts, touching me and pulling on me. A couple were burnt up like Freddy Krueger."

"Sounds interesting," I humored him, "but we both have planes to catch in a few hours. Let's get some breakfast, get rid of the car and get over to the airport. I have about ninety dollars left; that should be enough."

We parked the Minnow one last time, in the Wal-Mart parking lot, then went inside to get a cheap pack of tube socks, two bottles of Windex and one bottle of ammonia. We unloaded the luggage, picked up all the trash from the seats and floors and sprayed a layer of Windex over the entire ride, inside and out.

With the socks around our hands, we wiped down every inch of the rental car. We weren't as concerned with the dirt and grime as we were with fingerprints and any trace amounts of DNA that could possibly be used to identify and apprehend us. Hank's love stains in the back seat were thoroughly doused with the ammonia. Before too long, it was almost as if no crime had ever taken place there.

"How long do you think it'll take for the rental car agency to get it back?" Hank asked as we disposed of the soggy socks and empty bottles in a trash can.

"Well," I explained, "I was sure to rent the car until the day after tomorrow. They probably won't run the credit card again until then. It'll be reported as stolen, insurance will take care of it, write it off as a business expense."

"Compliments of Mr. Victor Zulu," Hank grinned while we collected our bags and trekked across the parking lot toward the Del Taco.

I treated Hank to some fine Mexican delicacies and ordered myself a tall stack of quesadillas. I didn't know when I'd see a Del Taco again and I wanted to make this special moment last. Then we called for a cab and waited in the parking lot.

Airport security wouldn't let me go through with the briefcase attached to my arm, but I had lost the key sometime the night before. A reluctant security guard was finally able to unlock my cuffs with his key and we were once again on our way through the metal detectors and x-ray machines.

Hank's flight was first, with mine to follow about an hour later from the same terminal. We made it to Hank's gate in just enough time for him to board.

"What do you say?" Hank asked as he shook my hand. "Same time next year?"

"Like a dog back to its vomit, so returns a fool to his folly."

Then the fool smiled, stepped back and turned to board his flight back home. With any luck, this would not be the last time I'd see Dr. Hank Matthews.

I wandered the terminal, never too far from my gate, but just enough to keep me on my feet. I wasn't ready to settle down just yet, even if I knew that sitting would be inevitable once they started calling for boarding passes. I don't know if I was anxious to be finally done with this botched vacation, or if I'd miss it once it was completely over. Likewise, I was finally going home to see my wife and kids, although it would be in New Jersey. It was all so bittersweet.

I noticed a couple of familiar faces in the distance, sitting down waiting at a nearby gate, and so I went in for a better look. The Magnificent Aaron and the woman he sawed in half were each reading a magazine, looking worn out from work and constant partying.

"I really thought you were dead," I said to the young lady once I approached them. "Man, you bled all over the place. I thought it was real."

"Just part of the show," Aaron said, never looking up from his reading.

"What about the rabbit?" I asked. "Did you really kill the rabbit?"

"What, this old thing?" Aaron unzipped his carry-on bag and produced a white furry lump. "It ain't real. I kill this poor bunny every week in a different town."

"You mean the whole thing was fake?"

"It's a magic show, man," Aaron scoffed. "Did you ever think a magic show was real?"

"But it was just gross; I thought you messed the whole thing up. It was awesome!"

"Yeah, that's my shtick," he sighed. "Everything's been done before. Even Criss Angel is just rehashing old tricks in new settings. Some people do funny magic, some people sing magic songs, other people make the Statue of Liberty disappear. The way I figure it, why bother? I half-ass learn the old familiar tricks, bumble through them and then gross people out with the blood and guts. I have to change my name at almost every show, just so people won't know what to expect, but at least they're surprised and entertained, even if they don't realize it at first. It's all show business, man."

"So, your name's not the Magnificent Aaron?"

"Shit, no, man. I'm Tim, and this here is my sister Amy."

"Your sister?" I was shocked. "So the whole thing was a sham?"

"No, it was just a magic show, and now you know all my tricks."

"You know," I confessed, "I really liked your show, but now that I know it was all fake, I just feel cheated."

"Well, I'm also Jewish and gay, just in case that'll disappoint you even further. That's what you get for bugging me while I'm reading my National Geographic. Now go bother someone else."

"So you liked all the blood and guts and death, but now you feel cheated when you find out I wasn't actually murdered on stage?" the magician's sister finally contributed to the conversation. "I think that says more about you than it does about us."

I remember standing on the pavement leading up to the Wynn, looking up at the beautiful structure and all that surrounded it. I remember saying to myself that it was all so perfect, because they had made it perfect. Even the gardening was immaculate.

Someone long ago had the idea to take this dried-up patch of desert and build an oasis there. There was absolutely nothing for miles and miles around, and so there was nobody and nothing to stand in the way of the dream.

It's always said that the grass is greener on the other side. It could be the other side of the fence or the other side of the world, but the deep and lush emerald carpet outside your door will never compare to what you picture in your head of someplace else.

As far as grass is concerned, I couldn't really complain. I'd always weed and feed a few times each season, and water daily in the spring and summer. My grass back in the Garden State is about as green as you'll find anywhere, and I knew that, but it still wasn't enough to satisfy me. Growing grass is easy, and I could grow it anywhere. What interests me is the dirt and the sand and the bedrock beneath it.

What the Wynn had wasn't even grass. It was AstroTurf. It looks nice from several feet away, but it's not until you actually step onto it that you realize that there's no give, no roots. It was all fake and nothing would ever grow from it. It was just another facade. That's all that Las Vegas really is. That's all it ever was.

But still, whether authentic or artificial, it was still grass, and throughout all four seasons, the grass in front of the Wynn would always be greener than my own, no matter how hard I worked in my own yard, wherever that yard may be.

The flight back into Texas for my short layover was quiet and uneventful, but the tired and angry passengers in the Dallas airport made the time stand still. There were children crying and running all around, knocking over other people's luggage. There were sweaty slobs in their greasy Wal-Mart best sprawled out on the seats instead of shelling out the cash for a hotel room. There was even a group of filthy hippies standing in a circle and kicking around a hacky sack.

I retrieved my cell phone from my pocket, found a seat at my gate and dialed the number to my house phone. My wife answered, and she sounded both relieved to hear my voice and bothered that it had been so long since my last call.

"I figured you probably decided to stay right there in Vegas," she half-joked.

"No, I'm at the airport in Dallas right now," I told her. "Do me a favor. Find a moving company and give them a call. We need to pack up and get the hell outta New Jersey."

"Really? And where do you think we're moving to?"

"I don't know just yet," I told her. "We'll figure all that out later. But stop watering the lawn. It's a waste of water."

I hung up the phone just as the man on the intercom called for boarding passes.

"Geez, where the hell did you get that black eye?" he asked as I handed him my pass.

"A funeral," I said, feeling neither the need nor the desire to explain further.

"A funeral? Where?"

"Las Vegas."

"Oh," he nodded, "Vegas." He seemed to understand.

EPILOGUE

You just can't trust folks nowadays to do what they say they're gonna do, and it's not necessarily because they're liars by nature. It's simply a common fact, and it's not even a modern construct.

There's very seldom ever a straight path in the journey around to the other side of the circle. Shortcuts are usually just short-term gains in distance, and then they almost always bring with them an unexpected increase in the number of tripping hazards along the trail. There are just inherent obligations that inevitably arise from time to time — distractions welcomed or otherwise.

Plans take a detour, time passes by at a much quicker pace than anticipated. Old dreams are left by the wayside to be remembered later on with longing and remorse and regret. Sometimes, rather, they're recalled as unfulfilled with contentment.

But it's all just time slipped away nonetheless, and there's no choice made when looking back from behind the eyes with wonderment in how it all got to be so far ago in the past.

How long has it been? How many years now? A decade? More? Shit....

But worse still, it seems, is that in addition to the untrustworthiness of people, places and things in this world are just as fickle, unreliable, temporary in their commitments.

In a city whose livelihood is dependent upon its ever-changing population of strangers, nobody notices just one more vagabond. In a locale where people flock with both a hope of winning big and a realistic expectation of losing some, no one pays any mind to yet another loser. It's not often here that a loose slip of legal tender in any denomination passes to a dirty palm from a slightly cleaner one, especially when there's no expected return in the exchange. Anything expendable has already been spent, and whatever's left is needed in order to get back home, back to normalcy, back to the obligations.

But for one particular stranger, normalcy has none of these distractions. He's living the dream, even if nobody else can recognize that fact in his appearance and actions.

He floats in like an apparition and claims a spot in front of the Chittenpük-On-The-Strip, a small low-key convenience store along the boulevard nestled between bars, eateries, tourist traps and casinos.

The one-stop-shop's neon sign advertises that it never closes. The posters taped to the windows let you know that it sells everything you could possible need from ice-cold Dr Pepper and exotic jerky snacks to sunburn cream and novelty t-shirts, that it offers discounted tall boy cans of piss-quality beer that can be hidden away in brown paper bags during hikes up and down the main drag.

With hollow eyes, the stranger observes people come and go, and very rarely does the same faces pretend not to notice him twice.

He watches as tall buildings are knocked down to make room for other tall buildings. He drags his holy leather boots across the litter of handbills advertising concerts, magic shows, breakfast specials and online city guides — most of which having long expired.

He's got life figured out. He knows what he needs, what he wants, and he knows just how to get it all. But most importantly, he knows what to avoid in life, though his opinions are greatly at odds with the general consensus.

He observes the running around, the dashing in and out, the flying this way and that. He thoroughly understands — but doesn't partake in — the rush to cram as much excitement as possible into a highlighted chunk of calendar as a means to get away from the normal, redundant hustle and grind, only to speed back at the end of the vacation to save up the funds and time required to plan out another similar future retreat.

Instead, he appreciates the opportunity to give up one surface of that particular coin if it means he can also forego the flipside.

So he gets by how he can, and he gets high when he's able. And when nobody seems to mind it very much, he'll drag his bare feet through someone else's green grass. He appears out of nowhere on a gentle breeze and he disappears again just as quietly and unnoticed. And from time to time, he'll hold a friendly palm out, extending the opportunity to make an easy selfless gesture.

Quarter for the men's room?